THE CYBORG'S STOWAWAY

IN THE STARS ROMANCE: GYPSY MOTH 2

EVE LANGLAIS

Copyright © 2018 Eve Langlais (registration no. 1147570)

Cover Art by Dreams2Media © 2018

Produced in Canada

Published by Eve Langlais

http://www.EveLanglais.com

E-ISBN-13: 978 177384 049 9

PRINT ISBN: 978 177384 050 5

CHAPTER 1

TRY NOT TO KILL ANYONE.

The order the captain sent Crank before they landed on La'zuun.

Kind of rude, if you asked him. There was no trying involved. Killing just happened, and he shouldn't be blamed. Folks—and even machinery— should be more careful about getting on his bad side. It probably didn't help he owned a pair of bad sides. One worse than the other.

The *Gypsy Moth*—that big, beautiful ship that he loved and hated in equal measure—landed without any intervention from him. Everything ran on automated sequences with only a little input from anyone. A crew of tolerable folk manned the actual controls and general upkeep of the ship's reactors. Since being made chief of engineering, Crank oversaw things for the most part. Barking out orders, keeping lazy shits in line.

Someone a few EC years ago—short for Earth Calendar, the regulated unit of time most human-run ships opted to use—had called Crank a conductor in the grand symphony that was space travel. He punched the fellow for making his job sound emasculating.

But he would note, he didn't kill the organic waste of space. The comment was tossed at Crank back in a time when he used the name Craig and only possessed *one* slightly bad side.

A lot had changed since then.

The ship finished landing with almost nary a jostle, the port they parked at a pit stop on the pleasure and vice planet of La'zuun. While the *Gypsy Moth* replenished, the captain and crew would conduct business. Flesh, vice, and goods. La'zuun appealed to a broad range of needs.

Crank would also be wrangling. He needed to ensure they topped up supplies—just common sense to always have a full hold, given the distance between planets with actual ports. Never knew when a streak drive might fail or an emergency strike. Mixed in the shipment there were also some parts needed for repairs. The problem with space ships? No sooner was one thing fixed than something else broke down. The real work in engineering wasn't the actual flying of the damned ship. Say hello to the glorified mechanics.

Who ran the ship.

Don't let those captains and lieutenants sitting in

chairs giving orders fool you. Without a functioning ship, they were nothing.

Which was why when he noticed Jameson—the captain everyone liked to ass-kiss—leaving the ship, Crank ignored him. Fucker.

Solanz approached, a virtual clipboard floating alongside her. She did so love her lists.

"Whatever it is, figure it out." He planted his hands on his hips.

"But—"

"You can do it."

"Sir—"

"Now I'm really not listening. Figure it out, Solanz." Her first name, not her rank. He did things differently in the bowels of *his* ship.

She went to open her mouth, and he grew quiet. Deadly. "I put you in charge. Can't you handle it?" The words had a hum to them, the result of him activating the FOZ protocol. Standing for Friends Only Zone, it was a small field projected from his wrist comm. It prevented eavesdropping, and lip reading.

And so long as he appeared to be giving her shit, people wouldn't know exactly what they discussed.

"Thought you should know, the city is in an uproar."

"When isn't it having a meltdown of some kind?" Busy planets always had a drama acting out.

"Somebody important has gone missing."

"Still don't care." He really didn't.

"Thought you should know since that will make them watch the cargo a little more closely."

That concerned him a little. It wouldn't do to have anyone find their contraband shipment of good ol' fashioned Earth whiskey.

Given its rarity, the Gaia Federation—which was the stupid name the humans chose when they decided they needed one formal government for their species—had forbidden its dissemination beyond Earth's galaxy. So, of course, it became a hot commodity.

Crank liked the taste of it. Almost strong enough for him to feel. He could drink a whole bottle and never get drunk. Another cyborg trait.

Some people thought his metal arm was the only thing that set him apart. His metal arm was only the visible part of it.

Inside, surfing his blood, embedded in every atom of his body, was nanotechnology. And not just the regular kind made in a factory. He had sentient bots.

They hummed inside him, repairing him when needed, keeping him strong. Alive.

Bastards. Sometimes a man didn't want to live. Stupid so-called friends never gave him a choice.

The machinery lowering the ramp creaked with a little more grinding of metal than he liked. He barked, "Have maintenance check the gears on that door." Keeping things in tiptop shape was crucial given the amount of time spent in space. Out there, the slightest pinprick of a hole could quickly balloon into a catastrophe.

Clunk. The ramp finished extending, the door opened, and he reached for his sidearm. His hand hit empty air. No gun strapped there. Not since the last incident. Captain's orders.

Fucking ensign should have known better than to sneak up on him.

The lack of weapon almost brought a hint of anxiety. He breathed through it. Kept himself calm and focused.

There was no threat. No enemy looking to remove him. But just in case, he'd hidden his arm earlier. Ordered his nanotechnology—via the chip melded into his brain—to camouflage his metal arm. It wasn't hard. Just involved pulling out a huge chunk of synthetic flesh. The bots in his hand went nuts.

The lump got absorbed and immediately broken down and reformed, spreading in a layer over the framework of his arm. The titanium steel rods wound with wires to simulate nerves and tubing of lubricant, a new kind of blood. The limb itself worked better than any ol' arm. The fingers were stronger, more dexterous. The whole arm was an improvement over the old.

But not everyone could handle seeing it. It brought back bad memories of the wars. The killing.

Not everyone forgave. Which meant layering skin over his metal parts. Hiding his greatness.

It bothered him. However, he'd heard of cyborgs

being taken. Not all of them, though. The regular kind that were truly flesh and machine were left alone. Only those with the nanobots ever seemed to disappear.

A documented five hundred and thirteen missing. Never heard from again. Crank had been keeping track, especially as their number dwindled. Asking questions. Even of himself. His bots weren't talking.

Someone was hunting them, and of late, he'd had dreams. A planet with a massive pool of glowing light, the motes in it dancing and talking. Until a shadow came over it. A beam of fire. Then nothing...

Dreams are for pussies. Cyborgs didn't dream.

Crank stomped down the ramp, his heavy boots sticking to the ground despite its light gravity.

Hands tucked behind his back, he barked out orders. "Hull squad, surface check." Six people, a mix of men and women, jogged down the ramp in pairs, goggles on. A tank was strapped to the back of one with a wand in hand while another carried the patching polymer. They'd repair any damage on the hull, the first layer of defense for a ship.

"Fueling crew, get your butts moving." The bellow brought forth the twins, Demetrii and Jemetraa, their gray hair tucked under caps. The fine skeins of the living metal filaments crowning their heads were in high demand with traders. But anyone who thought to grab the duo DJ would find themselves regretting it. They might be dumbasses, but they were Crank's dumbasses.

The pair scurried off to refuel, and a pair of burly ensigns followed to protect them.

Why the fuel? While the *Gypsy Moth* had the technology to renew their energy core over time, it could be a long process and deadly if they needed too much power at once and found themselves running dry. Dual sources were the smart way to go.

Crank kept belting out orders. Not really necessary. Like any well-oiled machine, his staff knew their jobs. He didn't tolerate any laggards.

Nor did he like strangers near his ship.

A quarter of the loading done, a squad of soldiers appeared, spilling out of a land cruiser.

He expanded the range of the FOZ protocol, keeping his expression gruff as he commanded, "Everyone keep working." Times like these, a wireless option like the ancient cyborgs used would have been useful. But technology to scramble those signals had been created and let loose, like a plague. Now to use it was like inviting certain death. It fried a cyborg's brain.

So they stuck to talking aloud. Unless they were trying to freak out the organics. Then they pretended to talk with their minds, their expressions stoic. Their lips shut tight.

And that was how the rumors started.

The port soldiers approached the loading bay doors of the ship. Crank grumbled as he stomped in their direction.

"What do you want?" he barked. No point in being

pleasant. He could tell he'd hate the guy in charge. And the one to the left of him. As for the other two... give him a few more seconds and he'd dislike them, too. "All our papers are in order. The merchandise has been paid for."

The lead soldier had a gangly three-legged walk, his sinuous shape slinking forward. Ugly fucker with his sallow yellow face pinched, his black orbs bobbing on stalks by his chin, his mouth higher up on his head, a gaping black maw lined in sharp teeth. One of his four arms extended. "Open it."

"Like fuck." Crank strode forward and stood in front of the box.

"Move aside, human. This is La'zuun business."

"Don't care about your business. This"—he pointed to the ship—"is my business."

"I have orders to search your cargo."

"My cargo was already searched back there." Crank jerked his head to indicate a checkpoint. The one he'd bribed to overlook a few items.

"Regardless, we have orders to search again."

Crank didn't immediately tell the fellow what he thought of those orders. That would come. He leaned against the hull of his ship and multi-tasked. He gestured to Solanz with his head. No need for words. She knew to check their special cargo was taken care of. To the soldier, he said, "What are you looking for?"

The bobbing eyes stopped and fixed him with a stare. "Have you seen a female?"

"Yeah."

The soldier straightened, his thick whiskers shivering in excitement. Crank drawled, "Seeing a few right now. There and there." He pointed to female crewmembers and even a planet-side dockhand.

Soldier Whiskers bristled. "I am speaking of a particular female. Have you seen this person?" The soldier flashed an image, the hologram appearing in the air above his palm, displaying a woman, her skin white as snow, long hair the bright green of summer, eyes huge and emerald, the makeup super ornate with loops and glitter. Add in a jewel in the side of her nose, strung with a filigree of chains that wound up to her ear. Attractive if you liked fey-looking women.

He didn't. Nor had he seen her. Crank shook his head. "Nope." Even if he had, he wouldn't have said shit.

"We are searching the boxes," Whiskers stated.

A reasonable request that Crank could easily agree to. After all, it wouldn't hurt for Whiskers to pop them open and take a peek. It was what Crank had planned to do soon as they were loaded. Always a good idea to check the merchandise.

But agreeing seemed too fucking cooperative and Crank wasn't really a cooperating kind of guy.

"You ain't searching my property. You see that there ship?" He gestured to the *Gypsy Moth*. "It is chartered under the Gaia Federation, which is a part of the Commonwealth." Which the ruling galactic body that kind of ran the universe. Kind of. Not all civilizations and organizations had agreed to sign on to having a governing force. But La'zuun was one of the planets that belonged, which was why Crank smiled. "Without a warrant, you have no legal jurisdiction to step on board."

Whiskers twitched, and he also began to protest, something along the lines of, "...be forced to arrest you for impeding..." Blah. Blah.

The gist was, either Crank obeyed or else.

Guess which option he preferred?

Sorry, Captain. Turns out I can't obey your last order. Crank flexed his fist, ready to swing, only the soldier's attention was drawn to a commotion over by the trains.

Shouts and running. Crank held his punch. Apparently, he didn't need it after all. Shame.

"Remain here until my return," admonished Whiskers before trotting off with his friends.

"Don't hold your breath about it," Crank muttered in reply. He spent a moment watching the last of the boxes emerging from the warehouse, ready for loading. Almost done and not a moment too soon. His gut said they might be taking off in a hurry.

Surveying the port, he admired the tidy hive-like efficiency happening around him. Things moved smoothly. Goods boarded and offloaded in a seamless rhythm. Keeping to a schedule.

He liked schedules. They could be packed with enough things that a man didn't have time for thinking.

In the distance, outside a warehouse, he noticed a blur. A distortion in the very air.

He blinked.

It's nothing. Just a trick of the eyes. Human eyes, he should add—because he'd opted out of the mechanical upgrade—prone to mistake.

Turning, he headed into the ship. Eyed all the huge crates. "Zane." No need to bellow, his voice carried.

"Yes, sir." The young ensign, new to the crew, saluted him. Academy habits took a while to break.

"Do I look like a fuckin' 'sir' to you, Zane?"

"No, s—. I mean, no, Crank."

While Crank ran a tight crew, he didn't stand for any of that grandstanding shit they taught in the military. Everyone had a job. Everyone was important. And he hated fucking titles.

Chief Engineer. Bah. Sir, double fucking bah. His name was Crank, even if he'd been born Craig Abrams.

Everyone he worked with was expected to use his name. Not some bogus fucking title. Yet, for some reason, the damned blockheads who worked with him had this habit of being respectful to the point of ridiculousness.

Their time in space near the reactor cores had obviously addled what little wits they had left.

Crank tapped the merchandise. "Open up these

boxes. Check them against our manifest and keep an eye open for a stowaway."

"What do we do if we find one?" Ensign Zane asked.

"Kill it." Because it never paid to be lenient to rats who snuck on board.

CHAPTER 2

"Don't kill her. We need her alive."

The voices sounded so close. Ghwenn closed her eyes and held her breath. Stilled the rapid flutter of her heart. *Quiet down.*

Everything inside her slowed.

The thick cloak she wore would hide her body heat, the threads of plumbum blocking any signals from penetrating. The fabric also masked her shape, so even if they did notice her, they might not realize she was who they looked for.

The steps moved away, and Ghwenn let out a pent-up breath. Close. Close to being captured and so close to escape.

She couldn't waste time. Every moment could mean the chance between success and failure. She needed to flee. Now. And not just this city, the planet.

The port for the ships visiting La'zuun was

massive, the Bazzr Port one of twelve on the planet and busy. Ships constantly landed and left, a steady stream of traffic she hoped to use to her advantage.

Currently, she hid in the export warehouse. The busy machine-run building was constantly receiving packages and bundling them for delivery to ships. Despite La'zuun's reputation for pleasurable adventures, trade also accounted for a good portion of everyday profit.

Ghwenn observed the many ships docked. A golden-hued one for the Bubyg hive. The queen had arrived with her consorts for the wedding. A Rhomanii citadel orb vessel hovered over the tarmac, its gleaming black exterior matte and yet mirroring.

There was a slave ship as well, the cages used for transport currently outside on the tarmac. Machinery rinsed and disinfected the boxes lined with bars and a few clear glass-like cubes, getting them ready for their next cargo run.

A massive vessel, its name boldly painted on its side—*Gypsy Moth*—was being loaded. The crates, moved by robotic means and overseen by humans, were large. Certainly large enough to smuggle herself aboard.

She almost went for it. Then a vehicle stopped and spilled out some soldiers.

Guess who they were looking for?

I am the most popular person on this planet right now. It wasn't a distinction she craved.

She needed to go. Now. There was no time to find a specific crate and climb inside. Ghwenn had to depart this planet. At this point—the point of desperation—just about any ship in port would do.

The cloak covered her as she stepped onto the tarmac. A clench of her fists and a whispered, "I'm invisible," helped her take a second step. Then a third. She felt as if everyone could see her. Any moment, someone would point.

Yell.

You can't see me. She whispered the words to the very ether around her. *Nothing here.*

She made it past the *Gypsy Moth*, almost having a moment of panic when her gaze met that of the towering man overseeing it. Giant among the other humans, his bald pate seemed at odds with the scruff along his jaw. The metal hoop in his ear gave him a rakish appearance. He wore a tunic with the sleeves torn clear. He surveyed things with a rapier gaze.

Their eyes locked.

He sees me.

Invisible. She held her breath. *It's nothing. Just a trick of the eyes.* She kept her fists clenched.

His glance shifted away. She let out her breath and scurried, heading not for any of the large ships but a small one that could be flown by one person.

She even knew all the codes to make it run. She'd learned them on the trip over. A trip where she'd been played for a fool.

I'm not blind anymore.

The sleek, emerald-colored vessel opened with the press of her hand on the hull.

"Welcome—"

She cut the computer off before it finished. "Prepare for departure."

"Pre-flight check in progress. Destination?" the dulcet voice asked, and Ghwenn had a moment of panic.

Where to? Where could she hide?

A limitless number of galaxies and planets. How to choose?

She knew of one that wouldn't turn her, a female, over to anyone. "Zonia." A planet of fierce warriors where the males had few rights and where their honor wouldn't allow them to hand Ghwenn to anyone, no matter how much they demanded—or threatened.

And there would be threats.

The computer began preparing the vessel for take-off. "Setting coordinates. Pressurizing the craft. It is advised that biological passengers take a seat and buckle themselves in."

The process for departure happened quickly. Just not fast enough to suit Ghwenn. How long before someone remarked on the ship preparing to leave? A ship that wasn't scheduled to depart for a few days.

As she sank into the navigator's seat, one of two in the smallish vessel, the summons came.

"Incoming communication from the Bazzr Port Authority."

It couldn't be avoided. "Put it through and present all replies in audio pattern F67." This would turn anything she said aloud into a specific voice that would pass any speech recognition program.

"*Emerald Spring*, you are not cleared for departure."

"Then clear me." She spoke the words in her voice, but she knew on the other end they heard a gruff man.

"Negative, *Emerald Spring*. We cannot clear you for departure. Due to a security issue, all vessels are to remain grounded."

"You think I don't know about your *issue*?" She gave the word a sneering twist. "It's *my* daughter that is missing," she snapped. "Because of your incompetence." Spat out much as her father would.

"Sorry, sir. But my orders—"

She cut him off. "I don't care about your orders. I have a tip on my daughter's location, which means I am going to depart this planet and I am going to find her worthless carcass. I would not advise you get in my way or you will suffer diplomatic consequences."

A brash threat to make. But totally in character. She shut off communications and huffed. Hopefully they would buy it. She kept prepping as if they were.

"Beginning our taxi." The ship's computer relayed every step of their journey in her soft monotone.

Ghwenn had to wonder if she'd announce their impending doom in the same calm manner.

"Elsa"—the ridiculous name given to the ship —"any weapons sighting on our ship?"

"No armament is currently showing any signs of activity. However, the Rhomanii citadel did send a drone earlier to scan the vessel."

Nosy bunch, those space gypsies. Ever since they'd found their home world and lost their prince, they'd been scouring the universe for a sign of him. She didn't grasp why they didn't just elect another.

The Bazzr port authority tower didn't give her verbal permission to leave; however Elsa showed confirmation on the screen. They were cleared for planetary takeoff.

The ship entered a runway. While some vessels took to the skies vertically, that kind of push required a lot of power. A horizontal run could give the same kind of boost for much less energy.

The *Emerald Spring* hummed loudly as the engines spun, hurtling them down the cleared lane. Ghwenn stared on screen at the lights as they blinked past on either side.

Her stomach dropped as the craft lifted and began angling away from the planet.

I'm doing it. She was escaping.

She didn't let elation curve her lips into a smile. Not yet. She'd not even cleared the atmosphere. Plenty of time for something to go wrong.

Sure enough, her screen flashed.

"Incoming message from the port authority," Elsa announced.

"Play it."

She expected many things. A command to return at once. A warning they would shoot and disable her craft. Instead, she got her father's voice.

"You disgrace the family with your cowardice."

She didn't reply. It wasn't cowardice to flee what he planned. As a matter of fact, it was probably the bravest thing she'd ever done.

"You won't escape," he hissed. "No matter where you go in this galaxy, I will find you."

Then she'd have to make sure she hid well. She shut off communication with the planet. No point in listening to threats. She'd made her choice. Now she had to survive it.

The ship popped free of the shell of the planet, the shuddering of acceleration and the pull of the atmosphere giving way to the sudden calmness of space. Rather than apply any kind of brakes like most ships did given the rather crowded airspace, the *Emerald Spring* kept accelerating, dodging the various obstacles in its way.

A good thing the vessel moved fast. The tractor beam that shot from the side of a giant spined ship jostled the tail of her craft, giving it a good rattle. Her fingers dug into the armrest of the chair as her small ship danced among the vessels crowding the area. Many of them turned, ready to converge on her.

Had Father broadcasted a reward for her capture? Surprising given he valued the family's privacy and wasn't one to advertise scandal. Then again, what bigger scandal could there be than a daughter fleeing the fate her father had arranged?

A pair of cruisers, big ones compared to hers, angled together, forming a wall in front of her, and yet the *Emerald Spring* kept speeding toward them.

"Elsa?" She couldn't help uttering the name of the ship's AI.

"Preparing to jump. In four, three..."

Ghwenn closed her eyes as it counted down to two, then one.

Zip.

Her stomach bottomed out. Her insides sloshed, and her ship hurtled suddenly into the void, a fold of space and time that allowed travel between galaxies that would have otherwise taken lifetimes to complete.

When her ship finally cruised to a normal pace five jumps later, Ghwenn unstrapped herself and ran for the nearest waste receptacle. She dumped the sparse contents of her stomach. That many jumps so quickly played havoc with the body, but it would ensure she'd lost anyone who tried to follow.

She spent the next few sleep cycles anxiously watching. She had enough juice left for one more jump. Fueling became a priority.

What she didn't count on was the difficulty she'd have. For one, she couldn't access her credits. Father would trace it. No credits meant she had to bargain with items on board. Which proved a mistake. Riches drew thieves. Thieves stole her ship, and she barely escaped with her life.

The freedom she'd fought so hard to achieve?

Short-lived.

CHAPTER 3

THANK fuck for the short layover at that shithole of a way station. Of late, it seemed every port they stopped into had some kind of commotion happening. Stricter inspection of cargo. Flaring tempers.

It had all started a few weeks ago at La'zuun and followed them.

The latest port had a stolen vessel being argued over by authorities and the pirates who claimed it. The entities with stern expressions were less concerned with the entrepreneurs who'd acquired the ship and more with where said pilot went. Someone wanted the thief of the slick, emerald-skinned craft.

The rumor mill at the docks claimed a father was looking for his daughter. The reward was sizable. Seemed like an awful lot of expense to go through for a runaway kid.

Crank stomped out onto the elevated platform that

gave him a view of the entire engineering section, what some called the bowels of the ship. He knew it for what it truly was. The brains and heart.

And they were beautiful.

The energy cores had an ethereal appearance to them. The power—contained within clear, diamond cylinders—went several stories high. They glowed, their color not on the human spectrum. Whatever it was, it made his nanobots very happy. It wasn't unusual to see those who'd truly gone 'borg stroking the exterior. Even leaning their faces against it.

Much like the nanotechnology that adopted them, the origin of the energy cores was alien in nature—and expensive. Luckily the cost came out of Captain Jameson's pocket, but Crank got to enjoy it.

Taking the stairs down to the lower level three at a time, Crank didn't bother greeting anyone. This was work time. Not a social event.

The main control area for the engine room was within sight of the energy cores— a circular hub, ringed in consoles. He strode amidst the crew bent over their stations, eyes scanning, fingers flying. Always work to be done.

"Chief!" Someone called for him overhead.

He didn't reply. He wasn't a pet you hollered at.

Ensign Zane trampled down the steps and ran to Crank. He then almost saluted. He tucked his hands behind his back before making that mistake. "There appears to be a problem with that last crate we ordered from La'zuun." Which contained silicia, an organic material that resembled a fluffy pile of leaves. Purple ones with hair-like filaments that were valuable in the creation of holochips for a variety of items.

"What the hell is wrong now?" Crank muttered as he stomped over. The La'zuun cargo should have been fine. They'd checked it at boarding.

"There's something alive in the crate." The ensign indicated with a pointed finger. "Should we shoot it?"

Alive after weeks of being in space? Probably a rodent. Pesky buggers were hard to kill. "Don't shoot." Firing into the silicia would destroy them. Given their cost, and the use he had for them, they couldn't afford to lose even a single one. "Is it a rat? A bacoon?" Which resembled the raccoons of old Earth but with spiked tails and much sharper teeth. Funny how the universe might be vast but certain bottom feeders existed in every culture.

"If it's a rat, then it's a big one," the ensign said as he kept pace with Crank. "There's a huge flat spot at the back. Didn't see nothing, but the feathers were moving. Something is in there."

"Get the inoculation kit ready." They kept a few in engineering at all times because of the rodent problem. Being in space didn't make the rats immune to disease, and humans were highly susceptible.

It didn't take long to make it to the cargo bay. The large space showed various stacks of boxes and pallets.

Strapped in so they wouldn't shift. In the middle of the room, the open crate. And no one watching it.

"Didn't you set guards on it?" he asked.

"Yes." Zane looked around. "I wonder where they went."

Probably for a snack. Or a nap.

A nap would be just perfect right about now.

Crank frowned. Nap in the middle of the workday?

"Check the cameras to see if your rodent escaped."

While Zane peeked at the logs, Crank stomped over to the open container, hands held loosely by his side. It wouldn't be the first time he caught a lively bugger, although if he did, he'd have to make sure he crushed it without spilling any blood. Blood and silicia didn't mix well.

"Nothing exited the box, Chief."

"And those left to guard?" Crank asked, crouching down to see if he could spot anything. Not a single leaf quivered.

Nothing to see. Move along.

He shook his head. It was probably hiding at the back, under all the fluffy leaves filling the space. He began to dig them out, gently scooping them behind him into a pile on either side.

Nothing there.

The thought was in his head, and yet his eyes disagreed. As the last of the leaves dropped low enough for him to see the very back, he spotted a shape.

Huddled in a cloak. Bigger than a pest. Wearing clothes, which meant it wasn't a rodent.

A stowaway. Worse kind of varmint there was.

"You," Crank barked. "Hiding in the crate. Get out here."

The hooded shape didn't move, but it did waver from sight.

Nothing to see. But you are getting very hungry.

He blinked. He could go for an old-fashioned wiener on a bun with sloppy condiments.

What a strange thought. "Let's go, whoever you are. Don't make me drag you out."

Slowly, the hood turned, and he saw straight through the shadows hiding the face to the giant, violet eyes inside.

Eyes that widened upon seeing him.

"Who are you?" he snapped.

The figure in the cloak didn't reply, and yet he could have sworn he heard someone whisper, *Your destiny.*

No mistaking the voice inside his head this time. The kind meant to control his thoughts. If there was one thing Crank wouldn't tolerate, it was mind games.

"Don't you fuck with my head. I said get your ass out here." He reached in and grabbed hold of an arm, noticing how slight it was. He yanked the figure free from the box, dragging it through the remaining silicia. Only once they cleared the container did he remove his grip.

Arms crossed, he stared down at the cloaked figure. "Who are you? How did you get on my ship?"

Those enormous violet eyes met his gaze. The shadowy cowl of the cloak hid most of the features. Only a pointed chin and a pink bottom lip peeked. "I seek sanctuary." *Help me.* The words were soft and fluttery. They curled around him, as if trying to bind his mind with cobwebs.

He glowered. "Stop that shit right now, missy. You want help you ask for it. You don't force it."

Already wide eyes grew bigger. "A million apologies, Commander."

A sneer broke free. "I ain't no commander. I work for a living. Name is Crank Abrams. Chief engineer on the *Gypsy Moth*."

"I am Ghwenn."

"Whatever. Don't care. March your ass this way."

She began to walk in the direction he indicated, her slight figure enveloped by the voluminous cloak. "I seek asylum."

"I'm sure you do. And you might have gotten it if you'd asked the proper way. I don't do favors for stowaways."

She whirled before the door that he opened with a slap of his hand. "I couldn't come to you via normal channels. You don't understand the danger I am in. Those who hunt me—"

"Will stop once we present them with your body." Maybe even claim a bounty if there was one out there.

"Body? I don't understand..." The words trailed as she glanced over her shoulder at the airlock he'd led her to. "You're planning to kill me." She said it with surprise.

"Kill implies I'm physically laying a hand on you. This is more just getting rid of the trash."

"But I don't want to die."

"Then you should have thought of that before stealing a berth on my ship."

"I told you I didn't have a choice. And by your own admission, you are not in charge of this ship." Her chin lifted, pointed and proud. "Take me to your captain."

"Captain's busy. Besides, I got jurisdiction down here, and I have a rule about stowaways."

"This is ridiculous. I demand a fair hearing with the owner of this vessel."

"Stowaways don't get to make demands."

She stomped her foot. "Then you leave me no choice." Her hand flung from her robe, the fingers long and straight, the nails blunt and unpainted. *"Kneel before me and obey my command."*

The force of the demand hit Crank like a wrecking ball. Literally stole the breath from him, which was impressive considering he had one synthetic lung.

It trembled through him, this need, this desire, to kneel. To bow his head and promise obeisance.

Perhaps if he didn't have so much metal running through his body it might have worked. Or she wasn't that strong. Either way he fought against her demand and instead grabbed hold of her, yanking her close.

Only when she stared up at him, those violet eyes frightened—her lips never once begging—did he feel something inside crack.

He didn't kneel for her.

Nope. He did something just as implausible.

He let her live.

CHAPTER 4

GHWENN PACED the cell given to her. Technically, it was an airlock, the same one the chief engineer had threatened to eject her from. But he never pressed the button.

A small mercy, which meant she had no idea what to expect. He'd certainly been angry when she'd tried to influence him.

And failed.

Fatigue, hunger, and stress had rendered her powers weak. She'd used them so much in her escape with little time to regenerate. Now, when she needed it most, she couldn't draw on it. She had to rely on the dubious mercy of a man whose cold gaze let her know he would have killed her without a second thought.

And yet, he will be important to me.

She looked upon the man towering over her and it was as if a clarion went off inside her. A certainty overcame her, one that insisted this man would play a part in her destiny—and she in his.

If he let her live long enough.

She paced, pivoting every four steps, the space not giving her much room to fret. Her view consisted of four walls, two with grills inset within, allowing for pressurization—or depressurization, depending. The exterior wall did have a window giving her a view of the outside. Not much to see. Distant stars. Definitely no safety to be found, only cold darkness.

The wall with the door back into the ship also possessed a window, currently shuttered. What happened on the other side? Beside the frame of the portal, a control panel that didn't respond when slapped. Which might have been a good thing given she'd hate to accidentally trigger the wrong door.

Step, step, step, turn. She hated being caged.

But it was still preferable to the alternative. Would he really have ejected her into space?

What kind of person ignored her plea for sanctuary?

The same one that fought back against her voice.

That just didn't happen. Not with biological creatures. Cognitive beings were especially vulnerable to her skill of compulsion. But he didn't succumb.

Why? Had she truly grown so weak, or was he just that strong?

Could be he'd used a rare mind shield. But she'd

not seen him wearing one. Usually they circled the forehead, disrupting attempts to control thoughts.

Whatever the case, he foiled her. Which intrigued to the point that he consumed her thoughts. She couldn't help picturing him. Big and frightening. The bulk of him pure muscle, the top of his head quite bare of hair. His countenance fierce.

He could crush her with one hand if he chose.

Instead he'd shoved her into an airlock and abandoned her.

An eternity passed. She spent it wondering if this was the end for her. All that running only to end up as space dust.

Better than dying as a pawn of her father's machinations.

When the whir of machinery occurred, she fought to not scurry for the door, rather choosing to slowly turn, hands clasped over her stomach, head and eyes downcast. A properly subservient look that she'd used on Father the times his temper got the better of him—which was often. A daughter did not disobey her father.

Until now.

"Hello." A smooth voice spoke, certainly not the gruff one of the man who'd put her in here.

She glanced upward and saw a new human sporting a brown complexion, his hair cropped close, matching his beard. He wore a dark uniform, the tunic fresh, free of adornment and rank. Yet there was something about his bearing, his very presence that shouted he was in charge.

On a hunch, she declared, "I seek asylum."

"So I hear. What makes you think I can grant it?"

"If you can't, then I wish to speak to the person in charge." She gave the words a little push, and the man smiled.

Not a reassuring one she might add. He didn't melt to her command. Didn't do anything other than get an amused glint in his eye.

The dark-skinned man in uniform tapped his head. "Metal plate. Your tricks won't work, and I see Crank didn't imagine it. You're a mind manipulator."

The fact that he recognized it so quickly made her realize she'd gravely erred. By using her power without thought, careless really, she'd given away her secret.

The question was, what would these people do with her? There was a reason her father bargained her life away. A reason why she was so coveted.

As a valuable object.

Not a person.

Despite having been caught, she kept her head high. No point in cowering now. "I apologize for having made an attempt to nudge you—"

"Nudge," the chief of engineering snorted as he shouldered his way in beside what she assumed was the captain. "Nice one."

She continued as if Abrams hadn't spoken. "I only did so because I am in grave peril."

"The fact you truly believe your life is in danger is why we're even talking. Give me a reason why I shouldn't eject you from the nearest air lock." The captain crossed his arms.

"I've done nothing to harm you and your crew. I pose no danger and just ask for asylum."

"For how long?"

The one question she couldn't really answer, but given the stern stare, she'd better create one. "I only seek passage until we reach a large port."

"Then what?" her captor rudely interrupted. "You ain't got nothing to your name. We searched the crate you were hiding in. Nothing but protein bar wrappers and an empty flask."

"I am not without resource."

"Then why didn't you use your resources at the refueling station we just departed?"

Why? Because her ship had got taken over by pirates and she'd narrowly escaped being sold into slavery by a pair of brothel guards who probably regretted attacking the frail young woman. Her suggestion they become whores in her place also had the added instruction that they not use lube.

Served them right. But she didn't dare say that aloud. Instead, she chose her words carefully. "I was accosted before I could make proper arrangements for an escort."

"What happened to your previous escort?" the

bald man asked, leaning across from her, arms crossed. She noted a band of metal around a finger.

"What makes you think I had an escort?"

"Pretty girls don't travel alone. What happened to them?"

The questions began to irritate. "Take a wild guess as to what happened." She'd left those guarding her behind to make her escape. "Will you help me or not? Because if you aren't then let's stop wasting time." Playing meek hadn't gotten her anywhere, and her patience began to wane.

"I'm good with flushing you out an airlock." At her glare, his lip almost quirked. Almost.

It set her off. "What a disagreeable person you are. And to think I'd heard humans vaunt themselves as one of the evolved races, taking care of their fellow kind."

"We do. Can your people say the same?" This time definite lip action from the rude human.

"At least my people don't treat their guests like barbarians."

"Only because you're so snotty you never have visitors."

"Why are you even here? Go away that I might speak with someone more civilized." She batted her lashes, looking her most innocent at the man with the dark skin. "Is there somewhere we could speak in private?"

"Mind games don't work. Going to try and shag the captain next?"

She wasn't quite sure what he meant by shag, but she could guess. Her lips flattened, mostly because he'd guessed her intent.

"Go away." She shot a dirty look at the current bane of her existence.

The cad rubbed his chin with a middle finger, and a definite smirk hovered around his lips.

She didn't recognize the gesture, but she had a feeling... She turned away from him to the other man. Abrams called him captain. Someone of rank who could help if she convinced him.

"Please, I need your help." Said in her most helpless tone.

The captain didn't melt at her wide-eyed gaze. "Who are you running from?"

If she said it aloud, there might not be any more discussion. They'd just flush her out the nearest airlock. However, the rumors floating around might have reached their ears. How could she discover exactly what they knew? "You're asking for an awful lot considering we're strangers." A weak excuse.

"Then let me introduce myself. Captain Kobrah Jameson, and this is Chief of Engineering, Craig Abrams."

"Crank," retorted the rude one.

"Is that on account you're old and crotchety?" She hoped the barb hit home.

"She's trouble. Let me flush her," Abrams grumbled.

"Maybe later." The captain fixed her with a stare that had her turtling in her hood, as if she could hide. "How long have you been hiding on my ship? Crank says he found you hiding in the silicia crate from La'zuun. But I'm going to wager you boarded after we picked those up."

"It was during your last rendezvous with the way station that I became a passenger."

"You snuck aboard," Abrams interjected.

"Approaching you directly would have proven detrimental to us both."

"So you're admitting by your very presence on my ship you might bring trouble." The captain latched onto the small revelation.

"No," was what she said when the real answer was yes.

She heard a snort. A deep sound from the chief engineer. "She's lying. Anyone can see she's just gonna bring a shit storm down on us. Do we really want to do that? Haven't you and that woman Damon married been harping on about the fact we need to be on our best behavior for this wedding party gig that we are grabbing at our next stop?"

Jameson frowned. "The contract for that one is tight. Huge payout for a successful trip. Big cuts in it if we don't. Crank is right. We can't afford any trouble."

"Especially for someone who still hasn't shown her

face. We don't even know *what* you are." The cyborg smirked.

What were the chances she could remain hidden inside her cloak?

She didn't want to show her face. What if they recognized her? What if they kept her alive to sell her later on?

Hmmm. That would work. So long as she lived, she could escape.

Her fingers clutched the edge of her hood and pulled it back. She knew what they would see. Her large eyes which, while similar to a human's, were larger and could glow in the dark if she willed them to. Her skin was paler than the sand slopes of the barren Salia planet, a world made entirely of salt. Her hair, a short-cropped mess of black spiked strands. Her ears, with their pointed tips, bare of jewelry. Her nostril had a simple stud in it. No ring for the merchant class. No chain of nobility linking it to her ear.

"You're a Driadalys maiden," Jameson exclaimed. His surprise understandable given they tended to be a very reclusive race.

"An elf," Crank snorted, using the more vulgar term for her kind. "Should have guessed. Sly bunch."

"We are not sly," she retorted. "It is not our fault that our superior genes are misunderstood by a race still considered in its youthful stage of existence."

"Are you implying we're unevolved?" Crank

exclaimed. "That's priceless coming from a woman who's probably hiding from her own family."

There it was, that disparagement again. Not that she could do much about it. She was in a position of supplicant. She needed their help, which meant, as much as she'd like to defend herself, she had to tread carefully.

It didn't help he was correct. She did hide from her father. But someone as uncouth as Crank would never understand the intricacies of a Driadalys family.

"What's your name?" Jameson asked.

"Ghwenn."

"Ghwenn who?" Crank snapped.

"Only the royal lines have second names."

At the explanation, the captain's gaze narrowed. It flicked to the single stud in her nose. Then her hair, which didn't match her eyes. Only purebreds could make that claim to fame.

"I need asylum to a new world. Will you please help me?" She tried to shove down her pride.

"No." The chief of engineering didn't even hesitate.

"I wasn't speaking to you." She glared.

"We could always dump her on the moon before Kluuma where we're supposed to pick up the wedding party," Jameson mused.

"That's a few days from now," Crank remarked. "You'll need to stash her in the brig."

At least he spoke of putting her somewhere. The

brig must be their guest quarters. She hoped they would have a cleansing unit to remove the grime of her recent exertions.

"Actually, the brig is full."

"How can it be full?" Crank exclaimed.

"The majority of them are still being repaired."

"How much damage did that Brtuski do when he busted out?"

"Enough," grumbled Jameson. "Which means we need to put her somewhere else."

"Shouldn't matter where so long as you lock her in." Crank eyed her. "We can't have her roaming the ship unattended."

"I mean you no harm," she said.

But they spoke on as if not hearing her. "I agree. She'll also need to be guarded."

"Guarded by who? You do recall she plays mind games."

Abrams would remind the captain of her ability. As if it were her fault biological manipulation was possible to those with weaker wills than hers.

"I promise to behave," she interjected. "I just want safety."

"And so do I," the captain said. "For my crew. Which is why, Crank, I am assigning you as her guard until we reach our destination."

"What?!"

CHAPTER 5

CRANK WASN'T the only one to yell. Even Ghwenn took issue with Jameson's command.

"Surely there is someone more suitable," she argued.

"Find someone else. I am not watching her lying little ass." Because it had to be tiny. Now that the hood had come down, he could see just how petite she was. Except for those eyes. Huge in her face. A bright contrast to her hair.

And a Driadalys, a fancy alien word for elf. They considered themselves a superior species, rarely inter-marrying with the other sentient races. Rich because of the exclusivity of the items they produced from the more than a hundred terra-formed planets they'd taken over. Each ruled by a specific family.

The last thing Crank wanted was to deal with one. "I need to speak with you, Captain," he growled, stomping out of the airlock, waiting for Jameson to join him before slamming the door shut. Wouldn't do to have her hear him and the captain fighting.

"I can't be watching over her while still attending my duties," Crank retorted.

"As you so kindly pointed out, she can wrap most of the minds on this ship around her little finger."

"I am sure there's others who could fight it off." For all he knew, it was his bots making him immune. One of his staff might be just as good. He wasn't the only one with the nanotechnology. There were three others.

"Could be there is someone. But here's the other problem. She's a female Driadalys. With mental powers. Which means she's worth a fortune."

"Only to a specific kind of buyer," Crank said, still reeling from his surprise that Jameson would even think of selling another person. Even an elf. "Did you want some names that might be interested?" Because he knew folk.

"I am not saying we should sell her," Jameson exclaimed. "Fuck me, I know you still hate me for what happened, but give me some fucking credit."

"I don't hate you." As much anymore. However, Crank still blamed the man for making him live instead of letting him die with his wife. "And don't get your boxers in a knot. You're the one who said she was worth a lot."

"She is, which might be a huge temptation to

someone else. Whereas I know you. You'd never sell another soul."

He wouldn't. Crank had this thing about slavery...

"Some say the Driadalys don't have a soul. It's why they live so long." Kind of like Crank. He'd lost most of his soul when his wife Sky died—and much of his fleshly body, too. Now he had mechanical parts with a guarantee that they would never wear out.

Not even his ticking heart.

"Even if you don't like the Driadalys, I know you wouldn't sell her, not after Fxoria."

Damn Jameson for reminding him. Who could forget the cages and the pleas of those captured? Releasing them and then giving them weapons pleased him almost as much as the screams of their captors.

"There's other people you trust. It doesn't have to be me." Crank didn't want to be chained to the elf.

"What if you and I are the only ones who are exempt from her power?"

"I am not staying locked in a room with her for two days."

"Never said you had to. You want to drag her on your rounds, go ahead, but you'll have to watch her closely. Make sure she doesn't stir up trouble in the minds of the crew."

"Worried about a mutiny?" Crank smirked. "If that ever happens, it won't be because of a sly elf maid, I guarantee you that. We are one." The rallying cry from when the cyborgs back in the late twenty-second

43

century revolted against their human masters. That was long ended, though. Now they co-existed, with humans becoming cyborg by choice and not because of military experiments.

Jameson clapped him on the back. "Nice try. I know you'll never be the one to lead a mutiny."

"Don't be so sure."

"I am sure because then you'd have to deal with all the crew's problems and they'd call you sir."

"They already do." Crank grimaced. "But you are right about the problems. You can keep the job. Bad enough wrangling the grunts down here, I don't need your soft upper deck crew to handle, too."

Jameson offered him a faint smile. "So it's settled then. You'll watch the stowaway."

"Aye. But I won't like it." And neither would she. After the captain left, he attended to a few matters before returning to the air lock. He wasn't in a hurry.

He opened the door and found the elf standing a few feet within, features set in a cross expression, arms folded over her chest.

"About time you returned. Have you made a decision? Will you grant me asylum?"

"Don't take that tone with me, pixie."

"I am not a pixie! Do you see wings?" She pointed to her back.

"Take off your robe if you want to prove it."

"I am not denuding myself for your entertainment."

"And you're deluding yourself if you think I actually want to see you naked. You're not my type."

"Neither are you," she hotly retorted.

"Sure are hot tempered like a pixie."

Her expression turned icy. "You are rude."

"What can I say?" Crank bared his teeth in his version of a smile. "You bring out the best in me, *pixie*." Yes, he goaded her deliberately.

Her hands flung in a gesture of irritation. "You are unbelievable. I demand to deal with someone else."

"Demand all you like. You're stuck with me. Captain's orders."

She shook her head. "That won't do. I shall speak with him."

"Or you could try shutting your mouth and not being a pain in the ass about it. You're alive. Against my recommendation, I might add."

"Why must you be so terribly boorish?"

"Part of my charm. Now, if you're done busting my balls, are you coming with me? Or are you going to stand there bitching some more? Because if you're just going to be harping away, then I can leave for a few more hours."

Her lips pressed tight. "There is no other choice?"

There was always another choice. There was a red button thirteen inches to his left that would quickly solve his problem. But then he'd have to write a report about it. Listen to some bitching. Just wasn't worth the trouble.

Yet.

"Captain ordered me to watch you, so we're both stuck," he drawled. "I'm gonna tell you right now, I don't recommend you try anything. No mind games with me or my crew. No killing me in my sleep or poisoning my food."

"I am not a criminal," she retorted hotly.

"Funny because you were hiding like one. Let's go."

He gestured her ahead of him, wanting her in his line of sight as they weaved through the various humming components of the ship's engine. A vessel this size had many different sections to control the various aspects. Engines for travel were only part of it. Heating and oxygenation of the vessel had their own sector. Food and item replication needed machines to pump the raw materials to the units. Gravity, that had its own mechanism. In a ship that housed the population of a small town, a good portion of the vessel was turned over to simple operation.

And nestled within the various components, crew quarters.

Crank didn't need to slap his hand on any console for the door to his room to open. It slid sideways into the wall at his approach.

He gestured. "Get in."

She strode inside, the skirt of her cloak billowing with each step. She went a few paces and stopped.

"This room appears occupied."

"Yup."

She whirled. "Are these your quarters?

"Yup." He stepped farther in. The door slid shut behind him. It would now only open for him.

"Where am I to reside?"

"Here." Was she slow?

"There is only one bed."

"Yup." He ignored her as he moved past. He had a routine after he completed his work shift for the day, and even alien pixies stowing aboard wouldn't keep him from it. Routine kept him sane during the tough days.

He stripped off his shirt and flung it into the recycling unit. Rather than wash clothing and waste resources on board, items like crew uniforms were dumped and broken down into the raw particles needed to create the ensemble anew.

A gasp erupted behind him. "What are you doing?"

"What's it look like I'm doing?"

"You would rape a guest seeking asylum?"

He shot a glance over his shoulder. "You're not a guest." As for rape...his cock only worked for one woman.

"Don't you dare touch me." The command hammered at his head, threaded with panic. Finally, something other than the arrogance she'd shown thus far.

He ignored the mental shoving. Just like he ignored

her sensibilities. Let her think he would do something. Maybe she'd show a little more respect. She should be afraid.

Some days Crank scared himself.

He kicked off his work boots, the one thing he didn't recycle. He'd bought them from an actual cobbler. They were specially made, and worn in. Much more comfortable than the stuff the clothing unit could produce.

His hands went to the waistband of his pants. He began to slide them down.

"This is most unseemly."

"Then stop looking. Ain't no one forcing you to ogle my body." She wouldn't ogle for long. The scars were a living reminder he'd lost his pretty days.

"You were in an accident." The bold statement confirmed she still stared.

Worse. She'd remarked on his scars. His shame.

He clenched his fists. He'd punched people for less. The urge to lash out pulsed inside him. Only one thing stopped him. Given her diminutive size, he'd kill her if he hit her.

Without replying, he entered the bathing chamber, sealing it shut behind him. Knowing there was nothing in that room she could use against him. He took his time under the decontamination rays, spinning slowly, letting them bathe every inch of his skin. Some preferred the feel of recycled water sluicing them. Inefficient waste. The invisible waves of particle energy that kissed his naked skin did much more to remove debris from the body. What it didn't do was remove turmoil from the mind.

His daily routine wasn't calming him as usual. He remained all too aware she lurked in the other room.

Probably looking for an exit.

She wouldn't find one. Crank had modified his room well during those absent hours. Removed all possible weaponry. Reprogrammed the door and the communications access in his room to his voice only.

The only thing she could do was order food and clothing.

So imagine his surprise when he exited his bathing chamber to see her doing the one thing he'd never counted on.

Sleeping in his bed.

CHAPTER 6

GHWENN AWOKE FEELING REFRESHED and rested. It had been a while since she'd enjoyed an uninterrupted period of slumber. During her escape, she'd woken at every tiny blip of the ship's computer. On the way station, she kept moving around lest someone find her. Even when she snuck aboard the *Gypsy Moth*, she slept in snatches, knowing she could be discovered at any time.

It was rather surprising she slept at all given the man they'd entrusted her to. Yet...his gruff nature, and his lack of interest in her, provided a rather soothing relief.

He truly wanted nothing to do with her. She might not be able to control his mind, but she could feel his disdain. Yet that wasn't the only thing lurking inside him. Abrams was in pain, too.

She wondered if it was on account of his scars.

They puckered the skin of his body. Badges of honor, or something else? Asking would probably result in him getting annoyed again. A constant state for him she'd wager.

As her limbs woke, she stretched in the big bed that no longer appeared so neat. When her jailor went to bathe, she'd eyed the tucked sheets. The single pillow. The mattress that seemed to whisper, "Ghwenn. Come and sleep on me."

There were many things she should have done. Looked for an escape route. A weapon.

She chose to rest.

Escape would only mean they'd lock her away more securely. And besides, where would she go?

As to a weapon? She had no interest in killing anyone. Unless someone tried to touch her. Which he hadn't. Her jailor had not come to bed at all.

I wonder where he slept?

Rolling over she let out a startled yell as she saw Abrams staring at her. The man crouched alongside the bed, dressed in a clean tunic and wearing a by now familiar scowl.

Pity, he could almost be handsome if you ignored the scars, the bald head, the fact that he had plain brown eyes, and oh, his humanity. There was a word for Driadalys that copulated with alien species. Disowned.

"You stole my bed," he grumbled.

"Did not. As you can see, it remains in the same

spot." She tucked her hands under her cheeks, snuggling into the pillow.

"*I* was supposed to sleep in the bed."

"You didn't mention that."

"My room. Should have been obvious." He glared.

"If you didn't like me in it, then you should have tossed me out." But he hadn't.

How interesting. The rude man should have had no problem dumping her on the floor, yet he hadn't. Why?

"Next time, I will," he announced, getting to his feet.

"Except there won't be a next time because you will have someone bring a second bed. We'll need some curtains, as well."

"Curtains for what? Ain't got no windows."

"For privacy, you dolt."

"Insulting me now, are you?" He simmered. She didn't need to read his emotions to see his body tensing.

She smirked. "You make it so easy." She pushed herself up to a sitting position. "What's for morning repast?"

"Get your own breakfast."

He turned away from her, his sleek jumpsuit molding to his body, snug in the thighs and across the broad shoulders.

"Since you have nothing prepared, then I shall bathe first."

Unlike him, she didn't parade her attributes. She entered the bathing chamber, closed the door, then stripped.

However, before she could enter the shower, she felt a change in the air.

She whirled to find Abrams standing in the doorway.

"What are you doing?" she squeaked.

"Keeping an eye on you to make sure you don't do something stupid."

"This is sexual harassment." Her hands flew to cover her intimate zones. Especially between her legs.

"Nothing sexual about it, pixie. Ain't got no interest in you. I'm married." He waggled his finger with its heavy metal band.

"I'm sure your wife wouldn't approve of you ogling a female who is bathing."

"I wouldn't be looking at you at all if you'd stop arguing and get in the damned unit. Move. Clean yourself. I ain't got all day."

She backed away from him, unable to turn and give her posterior. She entered the cleansing stall and lost sight of Abrams as the unit sealed shut.

Once the unit finished cycling and her skin tingled, she stepped out to find him gone, but a loose robe woven of dull gray thread lay on the countertop. She popped it over her head, the sleeves of it long, the hem even longer. It tangled in her feet as she entered the main bedroom area.

She immediately noted him sitting at a table. Two trays before him.

So much for his claim she could get her own food.

He pointed. "Sit."

Hunger had her obeying. She tore into the strange meal, not recognizing the cuisine but enjoying it nonetheless. Especially a salty strip of meat. It tasted especially good drizzled with a sugary syrup.

Once done, he wiped his mouth, cleared their trays —she having finished long before him—and announced, "Time to get to work."

"Bye." She waved at him, only to yelp when he grabbed her wrist. "What are you doing?"

"You're coming with me."

"Why? Just leave me in the room."

"I am not leaving you here to plot. Can't watch you if I can't see you." He pulled a thin cord from his pocket and began winding it around her wrist, securing it snugly before tying it to his belt.

Leashed. Like a pet. She tugged. "You can't be serious about this. I am not an animal."

"Says you. You want me to trust you, then you're gonna have to prove yourself."

"By following you around obediently? I feel sorry for your wife."

The words snapped him, and she found herself forcibly slammed against a wall. The breath huffed out of her as he held her dangling.

His lips pulled into a snarl. "Don't talk about my wife."

She couldn't reply, but her wide eyes must have satisfied him because he released her, and she heaved in a huge breath.

Smart would have been biting any further retort. Where he was concerned, she lost all her wits.

"When I return to my world, I see we'll have to adjust our entry on humans. You're not as nice a race as you've been portrayed," she subtly insulted.

"Don't you mean we're not all suckers?" He sneered. "How's it feel not being able to control what people think of you?"

She couldn't admit she found it rather fascinating. From a young age, she discovered she could manipulate those around her. Father and a few others being the exception. She could always get what she wanted.

It might have led to her being spoiled.

She angled her chin. "People can think what they like. You are making the rather wrong assumption that I care."

"Then that makes two of us. Let's go." He yanked on the tether as he headed for the door, only she dug her heels in.

"I can't go out like this."

"Like what? You're wearing a robe."

"That doesn't fit." Not to mention it lacked undergarments. It was downright unthinkable she exit into any public areas so inadequately clothed.

"It covers you. That's the important part."

"It is practically see-through."

He squinted. "No, it's not."

"I need shoes." She lifted the skirt and poked her foot at him.

"Your old ones are kicking around here." He ducked and reached under a desk area, dragging them out.

"I insist you properly clothe me."

"Captain said I had to watch you, not be your personal valet. So stop your bitching, get your shoes on, and let's go."

"No." Since she couldn't use mind tricks against him, she had to resort to other means.

She sat down.

He blinked at her. "I will drag you."

She threw herself sideways and wrapped her arms around the column supporting the table.

"Seriously?" He sighed. He yanked on the rope.

She closed her eyes and concentrated.

Strength.

Her muscles tensed.

He tugged again. "What the fuck are you doing?"

Unwavering strength.

She might have kept the mantra going forever if he'd not straddled her. Her concentration broke as she opened her eyes to see him over her body, reaching for her laced fingers.

"Get off me," she squealed. Never mind he didn't

mean his actions sexually, she reacted. Letting go of her own volition, she pummeled at him and her legs thrashed. She shoved at him.

Might as well shove at a boulder.

He didn't budge, but he did stare at her.

She stilled beneath him.

"How did you do that?" he asked.

"Do what?"

"Get strong enough to hold on."

"You can't seriously expect me to spill all my secrets."

His expression twisted. "And this is why you can't be trusted."

He went to lever himself upward, off her, and some instinct had her flinging her arms around his neck. She hung on to him.

"What are you doing?" He froze, his discomfort palpable.

"Sticking close. It is what you ordered."

"Not that close." He sat and went to pry her arms away.

Strength.

He pulled, but she held on.

"Let go, pixie," he growled.

With her seated in his lap, her face loomed near his. "But you were the one who said I had to remain close. Is this close enough?"

"I know what you're doing." Abrams turned from her. "It won't work."

"What won't work?" she whispered against his jawline, acting rather immodestly, but she didn't fear for her virtue. He'd made it clear he honored his wife, which made his discomfort at her proximity all the sweeter.

She squirmed in his lap, letting the robe ride up her bare legs. Noticing his eyes shifting to them.

It wasn't the only thing that shifted.

Her gaze widened in mock outrage. "That is a most unseemly reaction for a married man. What would your wife think?"

As expected, the words made him snap. He shoved her roughly from his lap. His abrupt stand yanked her arm upward.

For a moment she thought he would drag her, but he used his hand to grab the rope and squeeze.

To her surprise the rope parted, smelling burnt, while a fine ash sifted down.

He stalked to the door and exited.

Victory. She wouldn't have to spend any time with him.

So wouldn't you know she missed him.

CHAPTER 7

CRANK LEFT his room in a foul mood. That mood did not improve as the day went on.

For one thing, the secondary power core required more maintenance than expected. They discovered a tiny fracture in the diamond chute, which meant repair involving more than a simple exterior patch. To fix it, they'd have to evacuate all the energy. Not a rapid process given they couldn't waste any power and had to wait for it to drain naturally. Only once they'd used up all that energy could they weld the crack shut, sand the unit smooth, then do a full cleanse before refilling it. All that meant they basically had only one power source for the next week or so. Not ideal on a ship this size with an upcoming mission.

That put him in a bad mood.

The fact that Solanz saluted him and stuttered, "Ss-s-ir," when he stomped into view aggravated him.

But the biggest reason for his ill humor was in his cabin.

Doing nothing.

At all.

Ghwenn sat on the bed. Knees pressed, hands on her thighs, eyes closed, meditating.

Probably trying to take over the mind of some unsuspecting sap nearby.

Never mind he wasn't even sure she was capable of doing that, it made the most sense. Why else act so serene? Why else wasn't she looking for a way to escape?

Why the fuck did he spy on her?

Captain said to keep an eye. That didn't mean he had to do it literally. He could just as easily rely on the monitoring systems in his room that kept track of a few things—motion, voices, heart rate. If something happened, he'd be notified.

Nothing did, though. So he kept tuning in, checking for himself. Spending more time than he liked staring.

He shut off the video feed and tried to concentrate on real work. Real things that mattered. Instead, he found himself toying with the ring on his finger.

Not the original one Sky had given him when they married. That one was long gone, along with his arm.

A day he couldn't forget. The day his life went to shit.

The planet had appeared benign by all reports.

Sandy beaches, warm waters, no large predators. A lovely place for a meeting between feuding rulers.

"I can't wait to hit the water." His wife twirled in their room, dressed in her uniform but dangling a skimpy bathing suit from a finger.

"You think the talks will go that well?" he asked, buckling his belt, feeling naked without a weapon in the holster

Sky scrunched her nose. *"A girl can hope."*

Hope was all they had for these peace negotiations. Captain Jameson and the Moth had been in charge of picking up the Rohmayo contingent while Jameson's wife, a captain in her own right—of the Yellow Spacemachine—had ensured the Juelyette group made an appearance.

Feuding families that would meet for the first time in centuries and broker a peace for the sake of two galaxies.

The two parties met under a pavilion to protect them from the burning rays of the sun. Everyone arrived unarmed, even the captains and their crews. These were peace talks. They weren't about to allow any misunderstandings to mar the outcome.

The two suns wobbled across the sky. Refreshments were brought and replenished numerous times as the two parties haggled.

Standing just outside the tent, Craig—because he'd yet to become the machine-man of the future—laced his fingers through Sky's and tugged.

"What are you doing?" she whispered.

"I thought you wanted to go for a swim."

"But we're supposed to stand guard." She bit her lower lip.

"From who?" No one else was around. The ship would notify them if anyone approached.

To a man only recently married, those were reasons plenty to abandon his post. He was enamored with his wife. From the moment they'd met to the whirlwind courtship. He'd never been happier.

Leaving the pavilion behind them, he pulled her into the hidden shadow of a dune only paces from the rolling waves of the ocean and kissed her. The taste of the gloss on her lips sweet. The touch of her hands on him sweeter.

Engrossed in her, he never heard the shifting of the sand or the splash of water. Never even knew of the threat that emerged.

Sky saw them first. "Beware. Attack!" She yelled the warning that day that saved the lives of many. Except the most important one.

"Fuck." He eyed the dunes for a weapon, anything to protect them.

He should have been watching the enemy.

"Craig!" Sky shoved at him and lunged, weaponless, at the amphibian creature who'd marched out of the waves. Brave. Stupid.

She took the long spear in the chest. It went through her. Punched out her back. He stared in shock at the sharp point. Then even more disbelief at the fist-sized hole left behind when the frog creature pulled it free.

It was a killing blow. But for a moment, Sky staggered, and her head turned. Her mouth opened. She whispered, "I love you."

Then hit the sand.

"No." The word whispered from him. "No. No!" The most terrible cry emerged from Craig as he barreled toward the spear holder. He batted aside the long tip, and when it swung back up, he grabbed it, and heaved, ripping it from frogman's grasp, flipping it, and driving it through its chest.

But the mercenary hadn't come alone. Five in total emerged from the waves that day. Or so the computer informed him later when he asked for details.

Five mercenaries hired by the Juelyettes, who had no interest in peace.

And the only reason they didn't succeed that day? Because a stupid man wanted to make out with his wife.

Craig threw himself at them, roaring in rage and grief. Hoping one of the attackers would strike the killing blow. Searing agony sliced at his shoulder, leaving it no better than a hunk of meat. He still had his other fist. He used it. He threw all his emotions at the mercenaries, but they didn't do him a favor and kill him.

They did hurt him though. Smashing him in the face.

The ribs.

Each blow welcomed. Each hit brought him closer to Sky.

He fully expected to die.

Wanted to die.

Craig sank to his knees on the sand. His vision clouded by blood. His body throbbing from numerous injuries. He toppled over onto the gritty grains, his face only inches from Sky, with her eyes still wide open in surprise.

"I'm coming, Sky."

It was what he'd hoped for.

Instead he awoke in the infirmary. Apparently, Jameson had saved the day. Sky's warning meant the captain had time to hustle the clients to safety, get rid of the remaining mercenaries, and emergency evac Craig's ass to the ship. When the doctors on board couldn't fix the damage, Jameson had Craig put in stasis and jumped to a galaxy that could.

The keepers of the tech, glorified nurses who had only one purpose—to dip applicants into the pool of nanobots seeking a host—saved Craig, even though he didn't want saving.

And Crank told Jameson that the first time he visited. "You should have let me die." He felt dead.

His heart was gone. Literally. The broken ribs had damaged it. He now owned a metal organ. A metal arm. Even a metal plate in his head. He lost all his hair, too, which, oddly enough, was the thing that made him break the mirror when they showed him how well they'd managed the scarring.

What did he care how he looked? He'd lost Sky, and he blamed Jameson. After all, it turned out it was Jameson's wife's ship that relayed their coordinates to the mercenaries, who then laid the attack.

He didn't care Jameson lost his wife that day, too. She escaped after her perfidy. But at least she lived.

While Sky didn't even get a decent burial. He never knew what happened to her body. Jameson hadn't stuck around to sort the dead because he wanted to save Crank.

Asshole.

The ring on his finger, that he twirled round and round, he had made the first year anniversary of her demise.

Years later and it hadn't left its spot.

But of late, he'd been toying with it.

It didn't help that Ivan, the ship's biologist, kept saying, "How long you going to keep holding on to the past?"

Used to be the answer never wavered. Forever.

Now...now he had a hard time picturing Sky's face.

But he had no problem seeing bright purple eyes.

Fucking mind control shit. Ghwenn had obviously done something to him. Why else would he be thinking of that stowaway?

He pushed himself up from the console where he monitored, startling Zane and Solanz.

"Sir? Is something wrong?"

"Stop fucking calling me that." He stomped away from his crew and didn't know where he was going until he stood in front of the door to his room.

Have you done something to me? Did she even now poison his thoughts?

He closed his eyes and listened, not with his ears. He checked for any kind of waves coming from his room. Scoured for even the faintest hint of a signal being broadcast.

Nothing.

He glanced at his wrist comm again.

Again! Dammit. Why would she not leave his mind? Did he have a virus? As a cyborg, he was capable of running a diagnostic. The tenth one emerged just as clean as the first.

Could his nanobots even recognize mind control? He certainly had before when it was directly aimed at him. However, searching for it now, he didn't feel a single tremble at the edges of his mind. That didn't mean she'd not done something to him.

And it needed to stop.

He entered his room, making no effort to be silent about it. She didn't move. Didn't open her eyes. Didn't acknowledge him in any way.

It bothered. He stomped some more.

She remained primly positioned on his bed.

"What are you doing?" he barked. Weaving a spell? Subtly influencing the crew to do her bidding?

Deviously inserting herself in his head to make him forget his vows?

Her eyes opened, their vivid color striking him anew. "I was meditating. Something you should try, given your temper."

"Ain't nothing wrong with my sparkling personality."

"If you say so." Spoken calmly without a hint of disdain and yet he felt it. Unbidden admiration filled him. It irritated the fuck out of him. He didn't want to like anything about the elf.

"Why haven't you eaten?" he barked, gesturing to the empty table. "You haven't had a thing since breakfast."

"How would you know? Have you been spying on me?"

"It's my job as your jailor to keep track." A great justification for his stalking.

"Why do you care whether or not I partake of a meal?" *It's not as if you like me.*

The words weren't spoken aloud, and yet he felt them brushing across his consciousness.

"I don't care. But I am in charge of you, and I won't have the captain accusing me of starving your scrawny ass."

Scrawny? Ha. That certainly didn't describe her perfect figure. The view of her, denuded for the shower, had burned itself on his retina. A lithe frame, handful of breasts, trim waist.

"When I require sustenance, then I will imbibe. My metabolism was slowed during my escape to stretch out my supplies."

She could do that? He'd thought that was only a trait those carrying nanobots enjoyed. Cyborgs weren't restricted to simply eating organics. They could refuel themselves with just about anything.

Curiosity made him ask, "Did you really think you could stay in that crate until our next docking?"

She tilted her head. "It was worth a try."

"What are you running from?" he asked suddenly.

"An untenable situation."

He made a leap of intuition. "Daddy wanted to marry you off?"

"Of a sort."

"Why not just say no?"

"One does not just say no to my father. He takes it rather poorly."

"Then get someone else to tell him for you."

"You make it sound so easy, but none would defy him."

"Because he's a bully. I know all about bullies."

"I am sure you do." Her glance let him know she assumed he spoke of himself.

He did. He knew how to push and shove and bark to get people to do as he asked. But he also never made them do something they couldn't or really didn't want to do.

"Who's the guy he wanted you to marry? Is he

chasing you as well?"

"Does it really matter? I am hunted and so I hide."

"Do you think hitting a new planet and getting a new identification will stop them?"

"No. Nothing short of my death or marriage will stop them from searching. This"—she tapped her head—"is too valuable to leave loose."

He moved around the room noting nothing out of place. "You didn't try and escape the room."

"Who says I didn't?" was her reply, followed by a soft laugh. "Let's say I did, where would I go? I know no one on your ship. There is nowhere to flee. You, at least, are a known, if rude, quantity. With you, I am relatively safe."

She thought herself safe with him? How little she knew. Crank had a very thin hold of his control at the moment. Worse than the possibility of him strangling her, though, was his urge to sweep her against him.

A protective instinct kept rumbling within. Trying to emerge.

He squashed it. "Don't think I'll be putting my life on the line for you, pixie. I really don't give a rat's ass what happens to you. I'd hand you over in a fucking instant if it would help my ship."

"Your language is rather vulgar."

"Says the woman who pokes at people's minds. I wouldn't be casting stones."

His communicator buzzed at his hip. He barked, "Listening."

The speakers embedded in the very ceiling of his room came to life. "Crank, we're heading down to the Nexus. You joining us for a drink?" Karson asked almost every night. Had been trying for years. Used to be he said yes, he and Sky going for a few cups with his friends. Crank had stopped going when Sky died.

He opened his mouth to say no, but Ghwenn beat him to it.

"I'm afraid your Mr. Abrams is occupied at the moment. Guarding a most vicious threat." And yes, she mocked him as she said it.

How dare she reply for him?

"Actually, I will join you for that drink. Down in a few. Close communication."

Ghwenn still smirked. "That's it. Run away."

"Who says I'm going alone? Better get changed, pixie."

"I am not going."

"And I say we are."

She lifted her pert nose. "You may leave. I will remain here."

"Now who's scared?"

Her lips pursed. "Why are you doing this?"

Why, indeed. It only occurred to him as he marched her down the halls—after an invigorating wrestling match he won—to the heart of the ship where the forbidden bar was hidden, that he was feeling something he'd not felt in a long time.

Alive.

CHAPTER 8

THE MAN WOULDN'T TAKE no for an answer. He even ordered her clothes from the replicator and then insisted she wear them.

He dangled the plain gray uniform. "Put this on."

She curled her lip in a disdain learned at her father's knee. "I am not changing."

"You can't wear that." He gestured to her robe. The same robe he'd thought adequate earlier that day.

"I am not changing because I am not going anywhere with you."

"Then I guess you can go naked."

Before she could grasp his intent, he'd leaned in and gripped the neckline of her loose gown.

It tore, easily, shredded from her body, leaving her screeching. "What is wrong with you?"

"Many things, pixie."

Her anger gave her the strength to hurl a compulsion against him. *"Leave. Now."*

But his mind didn't cave to her demand. A slow smile curved his lips, gave his granite countenance a rugged handsomeness despite the wicked glint. "I'll go, but you're coming with me, pixie. Your choice, naked or..." He dangled the gray suit.

Lips pursed, she snatched it from him and tossed it over her shoulder. She planted her hands on her hips. Nudity wasn't a comfortable state for her. She endured it because it discomfited him even more. Ruddy color infused the tops of his cheeks. He kept his gaze trained high. His fists clenched at his sides.

Did she sense a hint of fear in his aura?

By all indications he feared looking at her. A man who respected his wedding vows?

Did such a thing exist?

In her culture, the majority of married couples enjoyed a hedonistic lifestyle. Part of being long-lived. Part of being evolved. Marital alliances weren't about anything so barbaric as love. Social advantage was always the goal.

Many contracts were accomplished when young and contained no exit clause.

But accidents happened.

Was it any wonder she had a jaundiced view of matrimony? But she did find his demeanor interesting. "Where is your wife?" Did there exist a possibility of her walking in?

"None of your damned business. Get the jumpsuit on."

"You're a bully."

"And you are trying my lack of patience." He glowered at her. Probably meant to be quite formidable.

She'd seen fiercer. She also didn't take orders from anyone. Especially a human. "Your brutish lack of control is not my problem. Perhaps you should think about self medicating."

"Perhaps I should put you over my fucking knee and spank you."

"Resorting to harm?" she retorted even as she could picture it. Her bottom presented, his hand raised to strike...only instead it caressed.

She shivered.

His nostrils flared. His eyes glowed for just a second. A bright flash of heat, and his feelings—for a moment they were unguarded.

Lust.

It hit her between the legs, instantly moistening her sex. Making her insides quiver.

A reminder that, despite their different species, they were utterly compatible.

She took a step closer. Close enough to smell him.

Pungent oil, clinging to his shirt. A male who actually worked. What a novel idea.

"Anyone ever teach you to respect the bubble?" he growled.

But he didn't move away.

How interesting.

"Why are you always so rude?" she asked, tilting her head to look at him. The tense line of his jaw fascinated.

"Why won't you just put on the fucking jumpsuit?"

"Make me." What she said accompanied by a mental image of his hands on her body.

She knew he received the message.

The shudder of lust in his aura, and the increasing heat of his body, hit her in a wave.

He stepped back finally.

"You really shouldn't do that."

"Do what?" she asked, a hint of a smile on her lips.

"I won't be seduced."

"Won't or can't? Is your wife really that special?" she asked.

His mouth opened. Shut. A myriad of expressions crossed his face until it landed on resolved. "Listen, pixie. You seem to forget I'm the one in charge here."

"Are you?" She advanced. *Touch me.*

"Stop it," he snarled as he lunged.

She didn't bother fighting. Not this time. She realized there was no point. Size gave him a huge advantage. No matter how she struggled, he could overpower her.

So she did something he didn't expect. She undulated into him as he snared her wrists. Pressed her body against his.

A sound rumbled through him. He released a hand to snare her jumpsuit.

Ghwenn moved with him, making sure to touch him at every turn.

He sat hard on the bed. Dragging her onto his lap.

Lifting a leg for him, she drew it back for him to slip on her pants. He said nothing. Didn't have to.

His body spoke for him.

The rigid proof under her bottom. Proof even he couldn't control.

He is attracted to me.

And yet he did nothing. He simply tugged on her pants, without taking any untoward advantage. He pulled up the suit and maneuvered her arms. He didn't even tickle her breasts in passing.

By the time they were done, he wasn't the only one breathing heavily. An odd thrill that made no sense passed through her.

It surprised her to find the jumpsuit he'd dressed her in quite comfortable. The material soft, and while it didn't cling tightly on the outside, her intimate parts felt snugly encased. Built in culottes and brassieres.

Now if only it came in a better color, and maybe with a few embellishments.

Abrams set Ghwenn on her feet. "Get your shoes on."

"I am still not going."

"Are you really going to keep embarrassing yourself by arguing?" He snared her shoes.

"Not arguing. Stating."

He advanced on her. Again, she didn't fight. She stood and lifted a foot.

"Seriously?" He arched a brow at her.

She arched one right back. Daring him.

His lips pressed into a tight line. But he dropped to his knees. Grabbed her foot in his hand, a firm grip. Skin to skin.

She stared down at the top of his head, expecting him to simply put on the shoes and stand. Instead, she felt the whispery brush of a thumb across her instep.

Her breath stuttered.

Their gazes met. Polarizing and shocking. Feelings hit her. Not just from him.

Something about him drew her. She reached out to touch his cheek.

His eyes widened then narrowed. He snapped his face from her questing fingers. A moment later, a rope went around her wrist.

Pulling it away did not release her. The tether remained snug around her arm.

The panic erupted. Fast and furious. She hated being tied. It reminded her of times her father forced her to sit by his side as he meted his cruel brand of justice. How she couldn't escape the cuffs when she flinched.

She whispered strength to herself and yanked.

"Don't bother, pixie. It's Flkliri rope. Strongest stuff around. It's not coming off until I say so."

"This is barbaric treatment." She tugged and scowled.

"Then file a complaint." Still on his knees, he grabbed her foot—roughly this time—and jammed a shoe on her foot.

It appeared as if she'd be going out. Tethered to Abrams, the short length of rope stretching between their wrists.

Despite the slack, she kept close to him. If she had to be stuck, then she might as well enjoy the tic jumping by his eye.

"Where are we going?" she asked as he tugged her through the door to the hall.

"Nexus."

"Which means absolutely nothing. And you know it. What is Nexus?"

"It's a bar."

"You're taking me to a tavern?" She didn't fake the incredulity.

"Tavern is giving it airs it doesn't have."

"It is a place to drink alcohol. Which I thought was banned on most charter vessels from Earth."

"It is."

"Why didn't you say so?" She moved away from him and quickened her stride. "I could use a beverage with a bit of kick."

"It's nothing fancy." Abrams kept pace, his stride longer and thus still more relaxed than hers.

"I am not surprised. I've seen some of your ship." Disdain tinted the words slightly.

"Don't insult my baby." He ran his free hand along the bulkhead, and she almost blinked at the softness in his voice and touch.

"You have affection for the vessel." First his wife and now an inanimate object?

"The *Moth* is special." He winked.

Abrams the grump. Winked.

The quiver of pleasure she felt was probably unseemly out in public.

Did he know? He turned from her and knocked at a nondescript door.

A screen on it lit, showing a pair of orbs. "What's the secret password?" it asked.

"Let me the fuck in or I'll have maintenance vent the lavatory lines again."

The door clicked and opened. Sound washed out.

She looked upon a strange place. A large area hollowed out amongst machinery and pallets of goods. Strung with a giant iridescent ball that spun from the high girder ceilings.

A wall with a ladder going up allowed access to platforms welded in place, sporting cushions for those lounging.

Others danced on the metal grate floor. Bodies gyrating. Heads back. Eyes closed. Mouths open.

Free.

As Abrams kept walking, she followed, more confused than ever that he'd brought her here.

This was a place of relaxation and he was anything but when around her.

Was she about to finally meet his wife? The female who managed to snare a male and keep him to herself. Quite the accomplishment. It made Ghwenn green with envy.

The minds around her were open. So very, very open. The emotions hit her in a wave.

Too much. Too quick. She tried to shut herself off. But the noise battered at her.

Lust. Happiness. Depression. Anger.

Everyone had something to express.

She stumbled.

Still moving, Abrams yanked her off balance, and the floor rushed to meet her.

Something halted her crash.

A mind that was closed off. Quiet. She latched onto it, and her hands grasped at the arms lifting her.

Who was this haven in a storm? Her hero.

She glanced up.

CHAPTER 9

HE WISHED she'd stop looking at him like that.

Crank already found it hard enough to ignore her. When she stared at him like that. As if...

I am someone special.

He'd forgotten how good it felt. How dare she make him remember.

The anger burned away the last of his guilt. Because when he'd felt her fall, off balance, he'd felt guilty.

Surprise. He hadn't thought himself still capable of it.

Fast reflexes meant he turned quick enough to catch her.

And then she looked at him.

Setting her on her feet, he dragged her to a table in the corner. And by drag, he meant he scowled at everyone in his path, and she, with a docile expression he hated, kept pace with him. Her hand resting on his arm.

The occupants of the table took one look at him and hastily removed themselves and their drinks. He parked her on a stool. Dragged the other close and sat, too.

"How did you do it?" she asked.

"Do what?" He slid his finger on the tabletop, the touchscreen illuminating the menu choices this evening. Since the replicators couldn't make booze, what they did have was distilled the old-fashioned way or bought in secret when they hit ports.

"Your mind. It's gone quiet."

She'd noticed. Good. It meant it worked.

"I am cyborg." A phrase that, to him, explained everything. He couldn't put into words or describe the science of how the nanobots accomplished things. Machine and yet sentient beings. They chose their hosts and then adapted them. Encouraged them to get parts that they could meld with their human flesh. Because, while the nanobots could repair, they couldn't create.

"I could feel you before."

Mention of the word "feel" brought a flash, a vision of her naked skin. Her lovely shape. His almost complete loss of control.

He'd begged his bots to do something. Anything.

They found a way to prevent her from using her mental projection. The subtle nudges against him stopped, but oddly enough, his attraction toward her didn't diminish.

"You won't be using your Jedi mind tricks on me, pixie."

"The Jedi are extinct."

"The Jedi are a fairy tale from Earth," he snorted as a drone arrived, a large platter bolted to the top of its humming, disk-shaped body. It hovered only long enough for him to grab the drinks.

Something pink and frou-frou for the woman. Something strong for him.

She snared his glass before he could explain this.

Ghwenn drained it. Then licked her lips of the clinging foam. "Weak. But palatable. Aren't you going to have a sip, too?" She pointed to the pink monstrosity.

He eyed it. "I'll order two more beers."

Before they arrived, some unfortunate faces did.

Karson dragged a stool over and sat across from him. "If it isn't a ghost. Nice to see you. And who is this?" His gaze turned to Ghwenn.

"She's no one. Just cargo the captain asked me to keep an eye on."

The ship's doctor raised a brow. "Since when do we transport live cargo? And how was I not informed?"

"I stowed away, and they found me. Now I am a prisoner." She tugged at the rope, dragging her hand up to show the tether.

Karson ogled the rope, then Crank, then her. He

then slapped the table. "You have some 'splaining to do."

It didn't take long. "Found her in a box. Dropping her at the next port."

"Since when do stowaways get the one-on-one treatment?"

"Because she's dangerous," Crank growled.

Karson leaned forward and smiled at Ghwenn. Did he not see the peril he courted?

Especially when she smiled back.

He almost punched Karson.

When the glazed look entered his old friend's eyes and he reached for the rope, Crank sighed even as his fist shot out and bopped Karson in the nose.

"What the fuck, Crank?" Karson reeled back.

But Crank paid him no mind and glared at Ghwenn. "I thought I said no mind tricks."

"Not my fault he was so transparent and easy to play with. I didn't do anything bad."

"You weren't supposed to do shit at all." He stood and yanked her with him.

"I told you I didn't want to come."

"And that's an excuse to misbehave?" he snapped as he threaded his way back to the door. Bad idea coming here. He'd had nothing but bad ideas since meeting her.

"Not my fault humans have the minds of simple animals."

She'd not seriously said that. He waited until

they'd exited Nexus and gone a ways down the hall before he turned on her. Shoved her against a wall, pinning her hands over her head.

"You will lose your haughty airs, pixie." The threat snarled from him.

"Or else what? You'll prove my point that you're barbarians?" The thin lift of her brow did nothing to abate his irritation.

"Keep pushing, pixie. Keep pushing and you'll see what happens."

"You won't disobey your captain."

"There's an old Earth expression. It's easier to say fuck it than ask for permission."

"If you insist."

Before he could stop her, she leaned up and kissed him.

Kill her. The panic hit him hard.

Kiss her. The desire surged within.

Kill her. Self-preservation and a duty to his wife demanded it.

Kiss her. Logic fled in the face of his arousal.

He couldn't say what he would have done if the lights hadn't gone out.

CHAPTER 10

SHE FROZE in the sudden dark, her lips pressed to his. The tension in his frame showed he was listening.

She listened, too.

Not only that, she eased out tendrils of her consciousness. Not as far as she'd like. Certainly not as far as her great-grandmother could, apparently. Ghwenn had only a fraction of the ability, and she sensed nothing. Not a single whisper of thought, which could mean only one thing.

"Assassins," she hissed. Their mind dampeners could foil her power. "Untie me."

There was no hesitation. He severed the tie and placed himself in front of her. "Stick close to me, pixie."

Only if it kept her safe. She'd learned the only person she could truly rely on was herself.

Despite the field dampening her power to influence, she still held a mental chant. "*Invisible.*"

It couldn't hurt.

She didn't hear a thing, and yet Abrams suddenly moved. She felt the passage of air as he threw himself to the side. The crack of something colliding.

Then the grunt of exertion.

Move. She gave herself a mental order and ran, away from the noise and the dampening field. Hands held out in front of her, she fled as quickly as she could, bumping into walls, her breathing harsh.

This blindness of eyes and spirit panicked her.

The lights came on in a sudden flood, and she blinked. Blinked and yet the assassin dressed in black, the swath of fabric around his face revealing only blue jewel-like eyes, didn't disappear.

Oh dear. Even worse, he wore a circlet at his brow, a personal emission field. It scrambled her attempts to control him.

So she kicked him instead.

The protection at his groin meant it didn't do much to hurt him. He lunged forward to grab her, and she ducked, dropping to the floor, spotting the sheath inside his boot. Her hand darted for a quick grab, the blade she retrieved short and yet sharp. She stabbed at the fabric over his knee.

It hit the flat edge of a protective plate. He twisted his leg, and she followed, dragging the blade until she felt an edge. She shoved, piercing between.

Not a sound emerged. A true assassin, silent no matter what. She wasn't, however, when he tangled a fist in her hair and pulled.

"Ow!" Outrage and pain combined.

There was a bellowed, "Get your fucking hands off her," then a wave of emotion. Foremost, rage.

Then it was her own admiration as Abrams attacked the assassin with no weapon but his fists.

Wham. Wham. He hammered over and over, striking the body armor and yet not flinching. Nor slowing. The assassin staggered under the assault. But this was no amateur.

The assassin recovered, spinning away from the devastating fists, emerging from that twirl with a knife that he flung.

Abrams didn't even try to avoid it. The knife hit him in the arm, sank into flesh. She gaped as she saw a red stain blooming from the site.

What did the fool man do? Cracked his knuckles, the sound loud, the smile louder. "Thanks. I needed a snack." The hilt of the knife suddenly fell to the floor minus the blade.

And then Abrams threw himself at the assassin. The circlet dampening his thoughts—preventing her influence—was knocked off.

This was her chance to read his... Nope. The body suddenly went limp.

Abrams cursed. "What the fuck? I barely touched him."

"Suicide," she stated, noting the clouding of the assassin's eyes.

"Suicide? Seems rather extreme given we would have simply jailed him."

"Capture is not an option." She knelt and pulled the scarf from the head, noting the tattooed features.

"He's an elf like you."

"Nothing like me," she stated, getting to her feet. "No one is. That's the problem."

CHAPTER 11

FOR THE FIRST time since he'd met Ghwenn, she had nothing to say. She remained silent while Crank arranged for the bodies—because a second assassin was recovered by the crew—to be taken to the morgue for processing. Both of them had killed themselves rather than be questioned.

Completely fucking psycho.

And elf girl had nothing to say about it.

She sat on his bed. Hands on her legs. Calm as could be.

"Captain wants me to report." Crank usually would have told him to fuck off, but truth was, he wanted a word with Jameson, too.

"Do not let me prevent you from doing your duty." She kept her words monotone.

"There will be guards stationed outside." The

assassins were dead, and yet the fact that they'd made it on board at all, and as far as they did, left him leery.

She didn't seem to care. She didn't reply.

He left, eyeballing the two ensigns. Both veterans. The circlets they'd taken from the bodies around their brows. "Don't open her door for nothing. No one goes in but me or the captain."

A crisply saluted, "Yes, sir," was the reply. The double gesture of respect brought a scowl that he wore all the way to the war room. At least that was what Crank called it. Large space off the command center where the captain held court. It was where they held meetings or got their dressing down. Usually Jameson, hands tucked behind his back, listing things he couldn't do; *No more telling the port commander he's a noodle-sucking vegetarian. No making the ensigns cry. No, you may not punch people if they take the last pudding when Ivan makes a batch.*

Crank didn't bother announcing himself and walked in. Already a crowd had gathered. The captain, arms crossed, glared at the wall screen of the morgue where the bodies were being robotically dissected. Einstein had parked her hover chair close to the table and leaned over it, gnarled hands flying. Damon also there, hologram in front of him, sound bubble around him, as he relayed orders. Given he was present, that meant Lazarine was off shift, probably sleeping before she had to work. Rounding out the group was Natalya, who had her hands busy at a console.

Jameson turned his gaze to Crank and barked, "How the fuck did those hired killers end up on my ship?"

It took but a nudge from Crank's wireless transmitter to get the computer screen to switch views. Images of the hull of the vessel appeared. "We found their craft affixed to the underside. It's equipped with a very high-tech cloaking device. Kept us from spotting it."

"And what about once they boarded? How is it not a single one of our detection systems noticed a pair of cloaked assassins wandering around? They're pretty fucking distinctive." Jameson didn't hide his anger. As captain, he took an infiltration personally.

"While the others were digging into their bodies looking for answers, I've got a team sifting their clothes." Crank had his best looking for any more toys like the circlets.

"What of our guest?"

"The stowaway did not sustain injury." He kept his words formal. Professional. Crank resisted the urge to check on her again. She was fine when he looked only moments ago. It didn't ease the knot in his stomach.

"Was she the target?"

"Probably." Why else wear something on their heads that emitted a dampening field that rendered even Crank's nanobots blind.

"Has she said who might be sending assassins after her?" Jameson asked.

"She hasn't said a fucking thing." Not even thank you.

"What the hell possessed you to be wandering around with her like that?" Jameson paced.

"Didn't realize it was a problem. It shouldn't have been."

No one expected an attack.

"Who is she really, and what kind of reward is being offered that they're willing to risk boarding the *Moth*?" Jameson mused aloud.

It was Einstein, their resident techy person, who answered. "There are no posted rewards currently on the Obsidian Exchange."

Jameson shook his head. "You wouldn't find Driadalys assassins on the exchange. They only work for their kind."

"I'll question Ghwenn." Ask her why someone would want to kill her.

Tell me who and I'll kill them first.

"Find out what she knows. Someone had the balls to invade my ship. I want names. Locations."

"This wouldn't have happened if we'd dumped the woman. It's not too late to do so still." Not too late for him. He'd not forgotten his vows to Sky.

Yet.

All eyes turned to Crank.

For some reason he shifted, as if uncomfortable.

"Why are you all staring at me? It makes the most sense."

"If you think getting rid of the elf is smartest, then why didn't you let the assassins have her?"

Because he'd seen red. Because danger appeared, and it was the incident with Sky all over again.

He couldn't let her die. But he could damned well get rid of her. "If we leave her ass on the next inhabited moon, we won't have to worry about more hired mercenaries."

"Only if they get the message in time. Were you planning to advertise the fact she was available for kidnapping?" Natalya's sarcasm matched her expression. The petite woman in charge of communication had slightly tanned skin and an exotic appearance, the bright mauve of her wide eyes offset by the gleaming blue buzz of her hair. She was also tough as the rivets on the hull.

"We are not ditching her somewhere she'll be trapped. It was our fault for being too complacent with our security. With the upcoming nuptial trip for our client, it's best we found out now. Wouldn't want the bride to be stolen."

Einstein snorted from her spot. "Steal her how? She's rather hard to hide if carting her around the halls." The Farras were a rather large mammalian creature said to resemble the extinct hippopotamus of Earth. Just as vicious when ill-tempered, too. Most people avoided irritating them, because it helped to stay alive.

Jameson didn't laugh. "The client believes a rival is going to try and stop the marriage from happening."

"A Farra can't exactly crawl around the maintenance tunnels on the ship. We'd notice them."

"A smart intruder will claim they're with the wedding party. Provide adequate identification and we'll never know the truth until too late." Einstein provided a plausible scenario. The darkest version of course.

"We will ensure that the entire wedding party is identified upon boarding," Damon claimed.

"They won't allow us to tag them or examine them too closely," the captain noted. "We will have to be subtle."

At least they were thinking. Crank tapped his wrist and took a peek at the screen that holographed onto his skin.

Ghwenn sat the same as before. Knees together, hands atop her thighs. Sitting straight, looking at a point left of the camera.

Hadn't moved at all.

As his finger moved to turn the screen off, there was motion. Ghwenn turned her head and stared right at him.

At least that was how it seemed. Yet she couldn't know where the camera hid. It was but a pinprick in size. Wicked nanotechnology. Expensive as shit. But the fact that he could run it without wires...

"...don't you think?"

The silence drew Crank's attention, and he switched off the camera to find everyone staring at him.

He'd missed something. Probably wouldn't have cared if he'd heard. So he put on his usual glare and grumped a, "Don't look at me. Whatever it is you want, I ain't doing it."

"You are to question our guest and report what she says."

"Rather not." He'd rather stay far, far away from her. The captain had no idea what he asked.

"Didn't ask if you wanted to." Jameson played captain in that moment, his gaze flinty and brooking no excuse. "You will speak to her and get some answers."

Speak? His tongue definitely wanted to get involved. It just might not be forming words.

Striding through the ship, his expression enough to scatter all in his way, Crank found himself twisting the ring on his finger. It had felt loose earlier. Now, he could barely turn it. It tightened like a noose.

A reminder.

You're married.

Technically a widower.

Who never stopped loving his wife.

Never would.

But Sky was gone and not coming back.

However, Crank was still here. He knew she

wouldn't want him mourning her forever. Yet how to stop the conflict in his heart?

The ensigns outside his door started to salute.

His finger shot out. "Go," he snapped.

"But—"

"Was I not clear the first time?" Deceptively calm words.

"The captain said—"

Crank grabbed one by the shirt and slammed him on the door. "Dismissed." He dropped him.

The ensigns scattered.

He paused a moment in front of the door and said, "Open up." The voice recognition unlocked the portal to his room.

A step over the threshold and he noticed Ghwenn had moved from her place on the bed.

Something hit him hard, and then she tried to run past him.

Seriously? He arm-barred her passage. She bounced off his arm and he let her hit the floor. Then glared at her. "And where do you think you're going, pixie?"

CHAPTER 12

GHWENN DIDN'T IMMEDIATELY REPLY, still catching her breath and huffing her irritation through the hair that flopped over her face. Her own fault really. She knew it wouldn't work the moment she tried.

The man was made of steel. Literally, given his cyborg parts.

He certainly seemed to prove it when the blow to his body did nothing and his arm shot out to block her before she could slip out the door.

As she sat on her haunches, pride and posterior bruised, she watched as freedom slid shut in front of her face.

"I asked where you were going." His voice emerged low and controlled.

"Somewhere safe."

He didn't make any effort to stifle his sarcasm. "Alone. Unguarded. In the open."

"Because it's so much better to be locked in a room, with nothing to defend myself and nowhere to hide." She raised a valid point and, judging by his tense posture, pricked his pride.

"There is no danger."

"Says you. For all I know you're an assassin in disguise."

At that, he raised a brow. "If I were, you'd already be dead. Which reminds me, don't hit me again."

"Why not? I doubt you felt it." To prove a point, she kicked him. Might as well slam her toes against a rock.

He didn't even flinch. "I said no hitting."

Because it amused, she raised her foot and nudged him. On purpose.

He dropped to his haunches, bringing his gaze level with hers. "My patience is not endless."

"Do the tiny robots controlling you not have a program for regulating it?"

"Does your mouth not possess an off switch?"

The riposte brought a smile. You'd almost think he'd been raised amongst the Driadalys courts. "Tell your ears to filter out my voice if it bothers you. I have no problem at all pretending you're not there." Saying that, she drew her legs into a crossed position and opened her hands and held them palms together, eyes closed.

She took in a few deep breaths.

Felt him staring.

Let him. As far as she was concerned, he wasn't there. Just her and an empty room, his heated gaze on her.

Or so she assumed.

What if he didn't stare at all? He could have even left. The man moved with the grace of a dancer.

Was she sitting here eyes closed for nothing? The more she wondered, the more the conviction grew. He'd left, and she was sitting like a statue. Looking like an idiot.

Her eyes flew open. She was startled by a pair boring into hers. Without thought, her hand flashed out.

Connected with a crack.

Ghwenn's mouth rounded in horror. "I thought you left."

"What did I say about hitting?"

"That you enjoyed it and I should do it more often?" she offered sweetly.

"I said no fucking thing."

"Are you sure? Because you're doing everything you can, it seems, to ensure I have no choice." Now that she'd found an argument, she threw it at him passionately. She scrambled to her feet that she might glare down at him.

"You're fucking nuts," he grumbled.

"Is that meant to be a cyborg compliment? On the lines of you'll be the bolt to my nut?" She peered down at her nether regions then his before meeting his gaze again.

A shocked and smoldering gaze.

"How did you manage to turn that into something sexual?"

Her lip curled. "You're a male. How did you not?"

"You know, for a minute, sometimes, I think you're a lady. Then you open your mouth and I realize you're no better than dock town trash."

"Funny, I think the same of you, except without the lady part. You're just a dock rat, through and through."

Rather than get nasty, he laughed. A rusty sound that boomed out, and while startling, it was contagious, too. She found herself smiling with him.

"You are something else, pixie."

"If you don't like it, then let me go."

"Go where?" He swept an arm. "Middle of some uninhabited galaxy. Not a single atmosphere you can breathe."

"But we should be arriving in a new star system within the next sleep cycle. There's a way station and even a vacation moon that you can deposit me on."

"Say I do, what will you do there? They are small, out-of-the-way locations. Not much traffic or opportunity." The voice of reason emerged from him and poked holes in her plan.

But that didn't mean she abandoned it. "I'll find something."

"You mean you'll play your mind games on inhabitants until they are doing your bidding. Gonna make them your slaves." His lip curled.

"Yes. What else would I do?" she asked in all seriousness.

"How about not use your power against folk because it's wrong?"

"How is it wrong? And how dare you, of all people, try and guilt me because I have a gift. Know right now, it won't work." She shook her head. "I have a skill. A rare one. And I am not apologizing for using it when it comes to protecting myself. Do you apologize every time you hit someone and break their bones?"

He snorted. "Course not."

"Yet you have a strength that is more than human. Abilities that are not natural. How come you are allowed to use your gifts and I am not?"

"Because you force people to do things against their will."

"And you don't do the same with threats and strength?" She curved her lips. "Because I recall someone forcing me into clothes, tying me to their wrist, and dragging me out to a tavern."

"That was different," he mumbled.

"Different how? You used your physical advantage over me to force me to do your bidding."

"I had orders—"

"I am not condemning you for it," she interrupted.

"You used your gift of strength. As you should. My gift is mental. When I use it, it's like doing the same thing."

He gaped at her. "No, it's not."

How couldn't he see they were one and the same? "So you're going to claim you're not controlling me right now?"

"It's not the same."

"Really?" She gestured this time. "Am I allowed to leave this room?"

"No. But it's for your own safety," he hastened to add.

"According to you. Yet, despite that supposed safety, you dragged me forth. Forced me into clothes of your choosing. Tied me. Paraded me like the basest of chattel."

"It wasn't like that. I wanted you nearby to keep an eye on you, and the rope was so you wouldn't escape."

"I can't escape you anyhow. You're immune to my mind tricks as you call them. I am your prisoner. You can do whatever you will with me."

He could do so many decadent things.

Ghwenn leaned in closer to him. Close enough to see the tic he couldn't stop. Such an odd mannerism for the cyborg to have.

A good thing he had it, too. With the wall blanketing out his emotions, she couldn't read him. Couldn't get the slightest hint of what he felt.

That very tautness, though, told her everything she needed.

She leaned closer. "Want to tie me up again?" *Then you can touch me anywhere you like.* She pushed the thought at him, and it hit the wall of his mind. Did he even get a hint of what she sent?

"One of these days, your insistence on using your power will get you killed."

"I am not going to hide what I am." She refused to hide in fear or shame anymore. Other races had what they called psychics. People versed in mind work. Perhaps she'd go live among them.

"If you don't hide, then you'll always be a target."

"Once upon a time, your kind was targeted, too." Humanity went on a purge trying to exterminate cyborgs once they realized they couldn't entirely control the alien nanobots they experimented with.

"Targeting led to killing," he pointed out.

"No one's trying to kill you now."

"It took centuries to reach that point."

Centuries that decimated a race. The nanobots that could make a cyborg live forever were few now. Ghwenn's history lessons of alien cultures had taught that, while the humans eventually came around and brokered a treaty with the cyborgs, the nanobots' ancient enemy—an enemy with no face or name because none were ever captured alive—could not be reasoned with. It was said that, despite the destruction of the Mothership of all ships, some of the enemy still scoured the universe, looking to kill the few nanobots that were left.

"I won't live under a rock."

"Then you won't live long," was his dire prediction.

"Care to wager? Although, I might warn, I hate losing and am not afraid to cheat."

His lips flattened. "You are the most irritating female."

"While you are a repressed liar."

Puzzlement creased his brow. "I don't lie."

"You have from the moment we met. You're not married." She watched his reaction as she announced it.

Judging by the tic, she'd struck a nerve.

"I am married."

"Where's your tattoo?" Because, while the ring was a symbol, the humans, following galactic custom, also got marked. A barbarian ritual branding themselves. But then again, who was to say that the Driadalys way was any better?

"I lost the tattoo in battle. But that changes nothing. I'm married." He glowered.

"You're a widower," she corrected. She'd gleaned that much from the minds in the tavern. The whispers she'd caught told how Abrams was rarely seen outside the engine room since the death of his wife.

He mourned her passing. It had a noble honor that intrigued.

In her world, a death meant a new beginning. A new alliance. There was no real period of grieving.

Whereas Abrams chose to remain alone.

It wasn't as if he didn't desire. She'd seen it now too often while he was in her presence to think him chaste. He lusted after Ghwenn, so why did he keep rejecting her? His culture allowed for casual coitus.

She reached up to cup his face, and he flinched.

But she wouldn't let him turn away. She held his face and stared at him.

"You actually loved your wife." Something almost unheard of in her world. It did exist, but rarely.

How did it feel? Her fluttery stomach wanted to know.

"I still do love her." He removed her hands and stifled the spreading heat in her.

Jealousy, hot and vicious, took its place. "She was beautiful."

"Gorgeous. Smart. Funny." He named off the martyr's attributes.

"What am I?" What did he think of her?

Rather than reply, he shot her a look. "Fishing for compliments now, are you, pixie?"

"I know you are attracted to me," she said, getting to her feet before twirling, the thinness of the gown she'd chosen to wear settling around her, at times clinging to a hip, a breast, teasing with her shape. The lessons learned in the flowery bowers with the matrons came in handy. When it came to making alliances, it was all about being noticed. She noticed how his gaze tracked her. She kept turning, employing the subtle art of the tease, just without the usual mind tricks. She'd almost had him before. A little more nudging and he would melt.

"I can see your devious mind whirring, pixie. It ain't going to work. Shake that ass all you want. I am not cheating on Sky."

"You can't cheat on the dead."

"First, I'd have to be tempted, and let me tell you, you're not half the woman she was."

The harshness of the statement froze her. Dropping all pretense, she whirled to face him. "Why do you insist on lying? You are attracted to me."

"So what if I am?" he practically snapped. "You're female. I'm a guy. It's chemical, means nothing. And I took care of it."

"What do you mean you took care of it?"

His lips curved into a cruel smile. "What do you think it means?"

He'd satisfied himself elsewhere.

With another female.

For some reason the idea of it hurt. She lashed out. "Why are you so cruel? What have I done for you to be such a—a—" She stumbled for the right word. He supplied it.

"Dick. You can say it like it is. I never promised to be nice. You're the one who is being pathetic throwing herself at me."

"Throwing myself?" She gaped. "I hate you."

Which was why she couldn't understand why her blood boiled at the sight of him. It didn't just boil through her veins but throbbed between her legs as well.

What was it about him that ignited her desire?

It made her angry that she lusted after a male with so little regard for her.

She paced away from him. "I can't wait until I can leave this ship."

"What's wrong, pixie? Did I hurt your feelings?"

Yes. Yes, he had. But she'd never admit it. "More like I'm tired of dealing with your boorish manners. It would seem your nanotechnology is defective."

"How do you figure? Everything is in tip-top working order."

"Except for your manners. They could use an upgrade." She tossed the barb at him with a triumphant smirk.

"You insulting my metal parts?" He held out his arm and flexed it, and it was then she noted the gleaming metal through the rips in the skin.

Immediately her irritation melted. "You're injured."

"It's nothing." He went to move, but she managed to grab hold of his arm.

She bent closer to look. "The dermal layer is damaged."

"Bots will fix it later. I just gotta get the right kind of nutrients first."

"How far does it extend?" She ran her finger from

the tear to the joint in his elbow then higher, feeling the flesh, real to the touch.

"Shoulder. But it's not my only replacement."

"You were grievously injured."

"Almost died. But they replaced all my broken bits and then had me introduced to a nanobot colony. One of them adopted me."

"And spread throughout your body." A symbiotic relationship. "Do you still feel?" she mused aloud, running her finger up and down his arm. Catching his shiver.

For some reason this caused him to tense up. His body became a rigid statue.

"I feel." He swallowed. "But I shouldn't." He drew his arm out of reach, and she noticed him twisting his wedding ring again.

A widower who still grieved. Who struggled with a promise to a ghost.

It only served to increase her fascination with him.

"So which port will you deposit me at?" She turned from him, hip giving a slight switch to work the fabric of her gown.

"Despite my recommendation, Captain says you stay aboard as planned. For now," Abrams admonished. "That might change if something else happens."

"Like what? More kidnappers? I can hardly prevent them, now can I?" A lilt of sarcasm in there.

"Someone is going through an awful lot of trouble to get to you. Assassins aren't cheap."

No, they weren't. But some things didn't have a cost too high. "It's about honor."

"Ain't no honor using someone else to do your dirty work."

"In my culture, it's considered more gauche to dirty your hands doing it yourself."

"Shitty system."

In that she couldn't entirely disagree. "My father will send more."

"Your dad's the one doing this?"

"I caused him great dishonor when I refused the alliance he arranged."

"Never heard of an elf pulling a runaway bride before."

Because it didn't usually happen. She whirled and caught the skirt of her gown before sitting on the chair. "My people don't broadcast their private affairs."

"Are they all as snooty as you?"

"No. Most are much worse," she replied with a smile.

"Can't abide pretension."

"Some would call it having manners."

"Fuck manners. Who needs them?" Turning from her, Abrams stripped off his shirt. Slabs of muscle drew her glance. The seamless appearance of his arm filled her with wonder. If not for the tear, you'd never know. Not a single line to show he wore a mechanical one. Odd, because elsewhere on his body, he bore scars.

"Why did the cyborg nanotechnology not heal the marks of your old injuries?"

"'Cause."

With that one syllable she knew why he had them still. They were a reminder. A tribute to his dead wife. A punishment because he'd lived.

His hands went to the waistband of his pants. She knew what he did. He was forcing her to look away. To not stare upon him.

The fabric slid down, and her eyes followed, over the thickness of his thighs. The tight calves. When he straightened to a standing position again, her gaze went to the spot between his thighs.

"I see the rumor is true." She didn't have to say which one, and yet he blushed.

She gaped at the surprising sight.

"I'm taking a shower," he barked before striding into the bathing chamber.

As if she'd let him hide.

She entered before the door slid shut. He immediately whirled. "What are you doing?"

"I wasn't done with you."

"I was. And this ain't right. Get out."

"What happened to 'fuck manners'?" She used his own vulgar words against him.

"I'm married."

"No, you're not. Not according to law."

"And?" He stomped into the shower. "I'm not looking to get hitched."

"Neither am I."

He turned to face her as the lasers did their thing and cleaned his body. "Are you propositioning me for sex?"

"What if I was?" What if she was being bold and going in blind?

She couldn't read his emotions. Couldn't read his thoughts. Could only feel and see. Even sight was restricted because he kept his expression locked tight.

She took a step closer. Reached out to touch his chest.

His fingers whipped around her wrist.

"Don't."

"What are you afraid of? You're a cyborg. Control yourself." She ran the tips of her fingers over his skin. The shell around him rippled. A hint of emotion seeped out. Wild. Lusty.

He was keeping it bottled inside. She flattened her palm against his flesh.

Soft and strong.

The feeling of it pulsed from her, and his flesh twitched.

"That wasn't a compulsion," he said, his voice gruff.

"Not everything I can do is about control. I can also read feelings and project them, too. It's considered especially pleasurable during sex."

"You've done this?"

"No." The intimacy of such a thing required trust,

and when you could read minds, that wasn't easily found. Until now.

Abrams provided an interesting dilemma. She couldn't read his mind. Could only judge him on his actions. On the surface they came across as brusque, and yet, she saw them for the mask they were.

A broken man seeking to wallow in his misery. Afraid he might be happy again.

"This is harassment," he remarked.

"By your human standards." She smiled. "In my culture it is known as the *luudo*. The flirting game."

"That kind of game can get you in trouble."

"I can handle trouble."

"Can you, pixie?" His sudden grab of her shoulders meant he could slam her with a bit of force against the wall. She gasped.

He leaned in close. "Do you understand what you're doing in tempting the cyborg?"

"So you admit I tempt you?" A breathily spoken inquiry.

"Yes, damn you. Damn. You." He said the words distinctly and roughly against her lips. He kissed her.

Pressed his mouth to hers and ignited her passion.

It simmered between them. Hot and encompassing. Their mouths moved in sensual rhythm, tasting and caressing. Their breaths joined as one, and their hearts raced with excitement.

He dropped to his knees, and she looked down,

watching as the jets in the atomic shower disintegrated her robe, leaving her bare to his view.

He stared for a moment. She feared he might run.

Instead he touched. He parted her thighs, wedging them open. His face buried between them, and she moaned at the hot breath fanning her sex.

She had to grab for him at the first lick.

The heat of it almost made her combust.

He lapped at her, his moist tongue working her most intimate folds. Tickling inside, finding her flower and stimulating it. He tasted her, and she let him.

She encouraged him. Her fingers ran over the bald pate of his head, feeling the energy thrumming, the restrained passion.

A mental coo of pleasure radiated from her as he lapped at her most intimate place. Stimulating her pleasure button. Making her clench in anticipation.

He thrust a finger into her. Two...

He pumped them as his tongue danced on her button. Flicking it as he pumped her in and out. But it was the vibration of his tongue and digits that sent her over the edge.

She clutched at him, gasping, as the climax hit her suddenly, leaving her trembling and spent.

He wasn't done.

He stood, so big. So strong.

She reached down and gripped him. The velvety steel length of his desire. It throbbed in her grip, and he uttered a groan.

Their gazes met, and he froze, froze even as the tip of him nudged the moist spot between her legs.

He would move no further.

"Why are you stopping?" She desperately craved what came next.

"I shouldn't be doing this."

Now, when her body was on fire, he had second thoughts?

She dug her fingers into his buttocks and pulled him closer. The tip of him pierced, enough to cause a tremor. "Don't you dare stop now."

He groaned again. "Fuck me, why can't I help myself?"

"Because it's our destiny."

Whatever held him back collapsed at her words. Along with her legs. Good thing his hands were there to hold her up, to pin her against the wall as he slid the thick steel of his shaft into her.

Stretching her. Claiming her sex in a way that had her gasping and clawing at him.

He took his time thrusting. Long, slow, deep strokes. Strokes that vibrated. He ground himself into her, the head of him hitting just the right spot.

Over and over.

Her pleasure coiled tight. His breathing remained even, and yet, the tenseness in him couldn't be hidden. When she climaxed, the muscles of her sex squeezing, pleasure exploded in her.

As it flooded her so did she shove it at him.

Feel it. Feel how you make me feel. She thrust it all at him. Tossed her essence against him, staining his aura with her own.

It triggered his orgasm, which, in turn, fed her own. A circle of bliss that kept giving and left them both panting.

Yes, even he panted.

She'd made him lose control.

The triumphant feeling brought a smile as she stroked him.

He tensed and then shoved away from her, exiting the bathing cubicle. Ghwenn was left to stare at his broad back.

Did he seriously abandon her?

"We didn't do anything wrong." Not entirely true. But, given he wasn't a pure Driadalys, the same rules probably didn't apply to him.

"Get dressed."

That was what he had to say after the pleasure they'd shared? "Back to being a dick, I see." She flung his own word at him.

He didn't reply, and she was too angry to let him simmer.

"Your wallowing in misery is commendable. After all, you are entirely to blame for your wife's death."

That earned her an angry glare. "What are you talking about?"

"I am talking about the fact you could have done more to save your wife."

His eyes blazed as he stalked back in her direction. "I did everything I could to save Sky."

"Yet you lived. She didn't." Intentional cruelty. The only weapon she had against his indifference.

"She died protecting me," he shouted. "She took a blow meant for me. I couldn't stop her."

"That's even worse, then," she said with a sneer. "She sacrificed her life for you, and this is how you're wasting it."

"I am not wasting—"

She sliced a hand to cut him off. "You are. Your wife gave you the most precious gift, and you're repaying it by being miserable." She yelled the words at him, chest heaving by the time she was done. "Do you really think she meant for you to live the rest of your life alone?" She hammered before he could say a thing. "Would you have expected her to remain a widow her entire life?"

"No. But—"

"No buts. You shame her with your attitude."

He stood stone still. "I never thought of it like that." He paused. "She... I..." He might have eventually spit out the words if the communication unit on his wrist hadn't gone off.

"Abrams." It was the captain.

"What?"

"You and the guest are to meet me in Corridor A Fifty-Seven as soon as possible."

"That's a docking corridor. Someone coming?" He

tapped at the wall in the bedroom, heedless of his nudity as he retrieved information.

"We have company. They hailed us only a moment ago when they came out of a jump."

A ship appeared on screen. Massive, emerald green, and accompanied by a fleet of smaller vessels.

Ghwenn clenched her fists by her sides.

"That's an elf ship," Abrams commented.

"A Driadalys escort has been sent to retrieve our guest."

"Pretty big fucking escort," Abrams retorted. "What is she, some rich dude's daughter?"

He cast her a glance, and she held her chin high as the captain revealed her secret.

"Apparently, we're in possession of Ghwennatha Rexterraesta, a princess of the summer planets."

"Princess?" Abrams roared.

CHAPTER 13

"I WAS GOING TO TELL YOU," she exclaimed as she skipped to keep pace with him.

Crank wasn't in the mood to listen. Bad enough a tiny slip of a woman had guilted him into realizing what a shit he'd made of the second chance Sky had given him. He'd slept with a fucking princess.

"You're a princess." The third time he'd repeated it.

"Yes."

"A royal elf."

"Yes."

Which was bad. So very, very bad. "Rumor has it that having sex with an elf princess is a death sentence."

"Not a rumor. My kind are very serious about keeping the bloodlines pure."

"Speaking of pure..." He glanced at her messy

mane of dark locks. "What color is your real hair?" Because unlike a human woman, she didn't have any bush to cover below.

"Does it matter?"

No, because he would have almost slept with her no matter the hue.

"A fucking princess." The snort of disgust was for himself.

"I don't know why you're so shocked. You said I was snooty."

"As an insult."

"Which makes it all the more delicious."

He tossed her a glare. "You're enjoying this, aren't you?"

"Yes. I've rarely run into anyone who thought it appropriate to treat me with disdain."

"Don't think because I know you're a princess that's going to change. I still ain't bowing to you."

"You already did."

The subtle reminder had him almost groaning aloud as he remembered the feel of her against his tongue. The scent. The pleasure...

His hand clenched tight—the human one—fingers digging into his palm. "You should have told me," he growled, still annoyed. Although he couldn't have said if it was because she'd lied to him or because they didn't get a chance to finish.

"If I had, you would have treated me differently."

"Fucking right." For starters, he wouldn't have

slept with her. But he had, and now he couldn't stop picturing it. Remembering it. Craving...her.

"How come your eyes are purple instead of green?" he asked. His history on the Driadalys might be thin, but he did know that royalty had specific eye colors. The Summer Land family being green.

"Eye shields." She paused long enough to pinch at the orbs, pulling off the lenses and revealing their true color.

Bright. Vivid. Green.

"All lies." He shook his head and kept walking, not even caring if she followed. Where would she run?

Around the corner, the hall widened into a receiving chamber. The pearlescent walls contrasted with the uniforms the crew wore. Unlike the Gaia Federation military ships, the crew on board the *Gypsy Moth* all wore one color. Black. It matched his mood.

Given the circumstances, Crank chose to wear his formal kit, which wasn't much different from his other clothing. Black shirt, with sleeves, paired with black trousers. It showed fewer stains—and blood. Good thing because he had a feeling some might be shed given the mood coursing through his being.

A fucking princess.

And the worst part was, he wanted to sink balls deep into her again. Wanted to feel...

No.

Not happening. He slammed a door on those thoughts. He would control himself.

As they neared, Jameson—dressed in dark trousers and matching tunic—turned to greet them.

"There's the stowaway princess." Jameson dismissed the crew he had been conversing with. "I should have known you weren't working class."

She tapped her nose. "Amazing how a simple omission can make you invisible." Royalty wore jewelry to mark their status.

"And the eyes." Jameson didn't miss the change. "I assume the hair is dyed."

She nodded. "My kind are too easily marked otherwise." For a moment, the brave face dropped and she looked with weary resignation at the closed docking bay doors. "I don't suppose there's still a chance I can change your mind about handing me over."

Jameson tucked his hands behind his back. "If you'd told me earlier, perhaps we could have done something to avoid this."

"I'd hoped to alter my situation before they caught up to me."

"Don't you mean hide?"

She didn't even look at Crank when he spoke. She kept her gaze on the captain. "Thank you for your hospitality." She turned and stood before the outer doors, hands clasped, that bloody serene expression on her face again. The one he couldn't read.

"What will happen to you?" Crank asked. Weak. But he wanted to know.

"My father will get his way."

"You mean he's going to marry you off. Surely the groom's not that bad."

Finally, her eyes met his. "In order to keep our bloodlines pure, my father has decreed I marry him."

The very idea shocked. "But that's—"

"Normal in my world."

"It's sick. He's your dad. You can't marry him."

However, she didn't reply. She'd turned her gaze once more to the doors, her expression Zen.

Crank didn't like it one bit. Not her resigned attitude or the fate she had to endure. He tugged the captain to the side. In a low voice, he said, "We can't just hand her over. It's sick."

Jameson spread his hands. "What else can I do? She's royalty. Unmarried royalty at that. I don't have a choice. We can't keep her."

No, because, as a pawn, she was much too valuable. Not only for her status but her mind power. "You're talking about condoning a life of being nothing more than a slave. Of..." He couldn't even say it. The very concept of it disgusting.

Whereas Jameson shrugged it off. "It is their culture. In ancient times on Earth, it was quite common in some royal families."

"It's fucking archaic and gross."

"She seems to have accepted it." Jameson angled his head at Ghwenn, who stood with her hands folded, patiently waiting.

A martyr to the slaughter.

A woman who, only a few hours ago, had clutched him inside her body. Blew his mind with a pleasure he'd never imagined.

"She's calm because she thinks there's no other choice," Crank grumbled.

"With good reason," the captain said softly. "She is the unmarried daughter of Daeron Rexterraesta. Not just a king but *the* king of the Driadalys. Any sign we're not cooperating and they will slaughter us."

"If he wanted to slaughter us, he should have sent a bigger army." Crank tapped his wrist and, in moments, projected a hologram in the space between them. The large emerald vessel and its zipping drones appeared. "Check it out. Look at the size of them. That's barely a skirmish. We could take them."

"We could, but at what cost in life?" Jameson held out his hands and balanced them side to side. "One life or many."

"What if she hired our services?" Crank cast for a solution.

"Her funds are tied to her father. They won't release them into her control until she is married."

"There has to be another way. Something we can do to help her." Because he really didn't like the way she acted all stoic. Pretending as if she didn't care.

Damn her for being brave.

The captain unfortunately noticed his turmoil. "Why, Crank, one would almost think you cared for the elf."

He glowered. "I don't." Didn't want to, was what he should have said. Yet something about the tiny woman had woken something in him. Something he thought had died.

Deep inside, he found traces of chivalry.

Crank racked his brain for an idea. One that wouldn't put holes in the *Gypsy Moth* or march a tiny woman off to a horrible fate. "You keep mentioning the fact she's unmarried. That obviously means something." Because she was definitely not a virgin. He jumped on that tidbit faster than a sanitation robot on dust. "What if we hitched her to someone?"

Jameson took on a pensive expression. "As a bride, she would automatically fall under different rules."

"Then it's settled." Crank clapped his hands. "Let's get her married and send the welcoming committee away."

"A fine plan, but who do you plan to marry her to? I can't. Still married, remember?" Jameson looked around. "Who does that leave?" The reception area was empty. Except for one other person.

No. Hell no.

You don't have to do something so abhorrent. I'll be fine.

The voice wasn't his own. He stared at Ghwenn, realizing she'd heard it all. The light above the docking doors pulsed as the pressure inside evened. Ghwenn held herself straight, chin high. The picture of acceptance. Was he the only one who felt her disappointment inside? The tremor of fear?

"Fuck me, I'll do it." Crank turned and cursed as he saw the captain smile. "You sly bastard." Jameson had planned this all along.

A theory reinforced when Jameson pulled a silver-colored stylus from a pouch at his belt. "Good thing I brought along my stamp to make it official. Gather around you two."

A crease between her brows, Ghwenn shook her head. "There's a reason I haven't married. Anyone who dares will become a target."

"I'm used to people wanting to kill me. So you'll need a better reason."

"How about you don't have to do this."

"I kind of have to." The taste of her on his tongue wouldn't let him do otherwise.

"It was only coitus. I never meant to trap you."

"Would you shut up?" Crank grabbed her by the hand. "We're getting married. And that's final."

"If you're both ready," Jameson interrupted.

"We are," Crank snapped, all too aware the light for the docking door had steadied. They were about to have company.

Jameson clapped his hands together. "Begin recording. Ship's log, Earth calendar year twenty-seven-fourteen, the two hundred and fifty-first day. We are gathered here today on the *Gypsy Moth* to join in matrimony Craig Abrams and Ghwennatha Rexterraesta."

"Can we skip to the short version?" Crank muttered as the doors to the docking area slid open. "We're about to have company." He saw the emerald ship within the bay, a ramp extending from it.

Jameson didn't move his eyes from them. "Will the couple clasp hands and repeat after me."

Crank already had a hold of one hand. He snared the other and faced Ghwenn. But she looked to the side. People in fancy robes were descending the gangway.

"Eyes on me, pixie," he murmured. "We've got this."

Jameson spoke quickly. "Repeat after me, I, Ghwennatha Rexterraesta, do take Craig Abrams to be my lawfully wedded partner until circumstances do us part."

She repeated, and then it was his turn. A roaring white noise covered Jameson's voice. The face before him wavered, Ghwenn, Sky, back to Ghwenn. Such a sense of déjà vu. He'd done this once before.

Last time he'd done it for love. And it crushed him.

He wouldn't let it happen again.

He was in control.

The words spilled out of him without him even consciously doing it. In a daze, he noted Ghwenn looking at him, waiting for something.

"...by the galactic powers vested in me as captain of

the *Gypsy Moth*, I declare you conjugal partners."
Jameson traced the stylus over their wrists, and a
tingling sensation hit his skin. "You may kiss to seal the
bargain."

"No," a stranger yelled. "We forbid it."

Forbid? Now someone was talking his kind of
language. Crank leaned in and pressed his mouth to
Ghwenn's, a tingle of awareness sweeping him.

Every time they touched he felt more alive.

Everyone would think he'd married Ghwenn to
save her. The real truth was he'd done it to save
himself.

A voice cleared itself loudly. "Ahem."

Breaking off the kiss, he met Ghwenn's clear green
eyes for a moment. She smiled.

Would you like to deal with them, husband?

A shiver went through him. Hell yeah, he would.
He straightened to face the newcomers with their
fancy robes and haughty expressions. His human arm
curled around his princess.

My princess. Fuck me.

The delegation came to a halt. The lead elf
appeared quite pissed, judging by the fact that a vein
throbbed on his temple. "What is the meaning
of this?"

Ghwenn held out her arm, showing off the fresh
tattoo on the inside of her wrist. "You can be the first to
congratulate us. We're married."

"Is it legally binding? There were no witnesses,"

Snot—Crank mentally nicknamed the lead elf because it suited him—argued.

"You saw it happen. And even better"—Crank pointed around them—"there are cameras and microphones everywhere recording not just my marriage to the princess here but this meeting."

Ignoring him, the lead delegate turned to Ghwenn. "Princess, since you have yet to consummate, an annulment will be easy to obtain."

"What if I don't want it annulled?" She snuggled into Crank's side. "I rather like the husband I found."

Crank knew it was an act, but for a moment, a part of him reveled in her claim.

"Your father—"

"Can suck it." She beamed. "Tell him he'll have to find a new wife."

"We shall relay your message." And that easily, too easily, the delegates whirled on their heels and began marching back to their ship.

Ghwenn tore free from his side and ran after them. "Hold on. I know my father. Why are you already giving in? You didn't even offer a bribe."

"Your father gave us our orders. We are simply following them." They continued boarding, forcing her to yell.

"So that's it? You're just leaving?"

"It would be foolish to remain aboard given what is about to happen."

"Which is?" Crank asked, having reached her side.

His wrist buzzed a moment before the emergency klaxons sounded.

Jameson barked, "Why is your lead vessel arming its weapons?"

The answer was obvious, and Snot confirmed it. "Our orders were clear. If the princess refuses to come, then she and all those who aid her are to be destroyed."

"You can't do that." Crank noticed the shock on Ghwenn's face then the determination. Despite not being the target, he heard the thought she thrust at them. *Belay that command.*

An order ignored. Snot turned to face her with a smirk. He dangled a charm. "Did you really think the king sent us unprepared?"

"You can't wear that thing forever," she snapped.

That was the problem with mind dampening fields. They could only be used in small doses lest they scramble brains permanently.

"We won't have to wear it at all once we destroy this ship."

Crank had no doubt they'd do it, and he could see it in her face. She knew it too. Pleading wouldn't change their orders. Her father would rather see her die than lose face.

So much for their short-lived marriage.

A decision had to be made. The *Moth* and all its crew or one confusing woman?

The choice was clear.

CHAPTER 14

DESTROY?

She knew her father would be angry, but she never expected this kind of retaliation. What would the captain do? What of Abrams? She couldn't read her new husband's face, and his emotions were locked down tight. Helplessness suffused her. The blaring sirens didn't help the situation.

Abrams stepped in front of her. Probably about to tell them what they could do with their threats.

"If she leaves with you now, will you promise to let the *Gypsy Moth* and its crew go?" Her new husband didn't even have the courage to look at her before offering her as a sacrifice.

"That can be arranged." Lord Kletuus, her father's closest advisor, agreed.

"Guess we don't have a choice then." He didn't even sound apologetic.

She stared at him in shock, and not because of what would happen to her. She'd been ready to volunteer to go with the delegates to save him, but to have him offer her? After he'd just married her?

He grabbed her by the upper arm and began marching her up the ramp.

She turned to hiss, "I can't believe you're giving me to them."

He leaned close and whispered, "Like fuck I am." The disdainful snort went well with his tone. "When I say move, hide."

Hide where? What was he planning? Did it matter? He had some kind of trickery planned that didn't involve handing her over. It was enough to keep her hope alive.

They reached the top of the ramp, the triumphant smile of Kletuus enough to clench her fists. How she wanted to wipe that smug expression. Instead, she tried to remain calm. Her husband asked for trust.

She gave it to him.

I trust you.

His fingers squeezed. "Now." The only word of warning he gave before he shoved her back down the ramp. He didn't follow. Rather, he uttered a bellow and dove inside the ship.

Was he insane? She paused mid-ramp as the captain bolted past her cursing, "Goddamn it, Crank. Why can't you ever stick to the fucking plan?"

Plan? They had a plan? Why did no one inform her of this plan?

Crash. What happened onboard the tiny ship?

She eschewed hiding and stepped toward the ramp, only to lunge off as a body came soaring out.

A slight stumble and she got her feet under her in the landing bay. Rather than return to the ship, she listened. She heard more bellowing, a high-pitched scream, and then another body landed atop the first. Followed by a third and fourth. Crank eventually emerged holding Kletuus, the leader of the delegation. He dangled the man, whose florid face matched the scrap of fabric shoved in his mouth, from one hand.

"Hey, pixie, how does your father feel about hostages?" Abrams asked.

As if they were expendable. However, the rest of the fleet wasn't as callous they soon discovered.

The armada of the Summer Planets and the *Gypsy Moth* entered a wary truce and began negotiating for the surrender of those being held captive.

There was anything but peace between her and Crank.

As he oversaw the removal of the prisoners to the brig, she harangued him. "Why didn't I know about your plan?" Why let her think he'd hand her over?

"Because."

"That's it? Because. You faked a marriage to me." She shook her arm at him, the tattoo on her skin a stark mockery.

"Actually, the ceremony was real. Had to be since we couldn't be sure if they'd managed to hack us. In case they were, we put on a convincing show."

All an act and he thought it amusing. She slapped his metal arm, which hurt her more than him.

He cast her a look. "Ow?"

"There is nothing entertaining about what you did. You've antagonized my father. Do you have any idea what he might do to you?"

"Kill me?" Crank offered.

A passing crewmember snorted. "If he wants to take a shot at the Chief, he'll need to get in line. Lots of people want to kill him."

"Bunch of whining pussies." Crank stomped after the crew who'd taken the prisoners. She grabbed hold of his arm. As if she could stop a walking behemoth.

He took a few paces before sighing.

"What now?"

"We're married."

"Technically. Captain will annul it as soon as he's sure we're out of danger."

"Or we could stay married," she boldly suggested.

"Why would I do that?"

"Because."

"That's not really an answer."

"I know." She couldn't give a proper answer as to why she wanted to stay married to this man.

This beautifully complex man.

Who'd gone through an elaborate hoax...for what?

133

Why the impromptu wedding if his plan all along was to hold the delegates hostage?

He left, and she paced the room they shared as she mulled it over. Trying to understand. Sure, the marriage gave Jameson the option to refuse to hand her over; yet, at the same time, they had to realize her father would never respect it.

As if he'd condone a marriage to a human.

Jameson had to know that. Surely even Crank did, too.

Truly their easier path was to send her on her way. Yet Crank refused.

He put the entire ship at risk for her.

Why?

When he entered the room a long while later...she was pretty sure she knew the answer.

Which was why she lay naked on the bed and muttered a husky, "I've been waiting. *Husband.*"

CHAPTER 15

"Put your clothes on." Not the words a red-blooded man should ever use when confronted with a gorgeous, naked woman.

"That will make it harder to consummate our marriage."

"There will be no consummation. I told you the captain is going to annul our marriage."

"What if I don't want him to?" She hopped to her knees and crawled to the edge of the bed, forcing him to avert his gaze.

"You don't want to be married to me." He was damaged goods. A man promised to another. A cyborg that had no business fucking royalty.

"Actually, I do want you as my husband. I can't think of a better choice."

"I'm not a fucking elf. I'm not even human anymore."

"No, you are cyborg, which makes you strong. And you are special, which is why you were chosen by the nanotech to survive."

"Obviously a defective batch," he hastily refuted.

"On the contrary, I think they made the right decision. You are very complex, *husband*."

There was that word again. A word that, for some reason, didn't draw the guilt he expected but rather a deepening hunger.

For his wife.

Not Sky. A woman he'd always love. But his wife here and now.

The one naked on his bed. Begging him to take her.

How could anyone think with such temptation on display? "Put some clothes on."

"Make me." She smiled. It was the kind of smile that promised wicked things.

Especially since they both knew he could force her to dress. But it would involve him getting close. The last time they were close he...

Sank into her welcoming heat. Moved inside her, their hearts and minds and even their damned souls— because he still had a fucking soul—moving in time.

What of Sky?

He twisted the ring on his finger. The loose ring.

Not even the one she'd given him, more a symbol of the past he kept trying to hold on to. He knew Ghwenn was right when she said Sky would not have wanted him to live in shadows forever.

"I'm not asking you to love me." *Not yet* was the whisper. "But if I am going to die no matter who I marry, then can't I at least choose who'll bed me? Can't I choose pleasure over pain?"

As if he'd let anyone hurt her. He didn't recall moving, and yet she was in his arms. Her frail form made to fit against him. Her luminous gaze mesmerizing.

"I won't let anyone hurt you."

"You can't promise that." *No one can protect me.*

The faint words weren't meant for pity. He wasn't sure he was supposed to hear them at all.

He wrapped her tighter against him. He wanted to lie to himself and blame his feelings for her on need. Pure and simple animal instinct to mate. To relieve himself.

What a big, fucking lie.

There was something happening between them. Something he couldn't deny.

He swept her into his arms. Crushed his mouth to hers, lifted her off the floor that he might plunder the sweet recess of her mouth.

Her legs wrapped around his waist, the most natural thing in the world. The heat of her pulsed against him.

He wanted to take it slow, to take his time.

But she drove him wild. The rake of her nails down his arms as he suckled her breasts, teasing each tip, the nipples finally their natural forest green color.

Everything about her was fresh.

He would have licked her to orgasm again. Planned to, but she wouldn't let him go down.

The compulsion teased at him. *Take me.* It didn't order. It begged. *Make me yours. Let me feel you inside me.*

The will wasn't there to resist. The head of him pressed, feeling the moistness of her core. There would be no turning back.

If he did this.

...then she'll be mine forever.

That sounded just fine to him. He thrust, and her nails dug as she cried out. She arched under him, her body bowing as he invaded her sheath.

He paused, giving her time to adjust. Her breathing went from ragged to soft and measured. The fingers stopped their deadly digging.

She relaxed and murmured, "More."

That he could do. He stoked her to the edge, letting his lips tug and his tongue lap at her sensitive nipples. He ground himself against her, stretching her channel, shoving deeper into her, not knowing if her kind enjoyed the same thing as a human. But given her increasing cries and the tightening of her sex, he did something she liked.

Her excitement drew his own, and his cock vibrated, pulsing within her channel, forcing her muscles to spasm around him.

Her hips began to rock in time with his, drawing him deeper, urging him on.

When his pleasure came, he gave a shout and spilled. Spilled inside her, and then he collapsed heavily on her body, the scent of her surrounding him. The heat of her flexing like a hot glove around his sated shaft.

It was good. Too good.

And the next time he took her was even better.

The third...

By the next morning Crank was in a foul mood.

He left his new wife, who smiled lazily from bed. He stomped around yelling at people, making a few ensigns cry until Jameson tracked him down and barked, "What the fuck is the matter with you? Would you just screw the woman already?"

"That's the problem," Crank snapped. "I did." He'd had a glorious night. And now when he thought of his wife... It wasn't a ghost he saw or a memory he craved.

Green eyes filled his mind.

CHAPTER 16

GHWENN DIDN'T UNDERSTAND her husband at all. He appeared so damned miserable. Barking at everyone in his way. Snarling, too. With her, he tried being cold and ignoring.

Which lasted only until she dropped her gown and laid herself bare.

Then he was on her like a hungry beast with a gentle touch, making her body sing. She knew he got pleasure, too, and the more pleasure he enjoyed, the surlier he got until she finally reached a point she was ready to snap. Especially since, every so often, the shield around his emotions dropped and she felt the reason why.

Guilt. He felt guilty for enjoying their time together. Guilt for caring.

He was letting a ghost come between them.

And she didn't know how to exorcise it.

But she had to do something soon. They were hours from docking at Kluuma and picking up this super important wedding party. They were still accompanied by her father's fleet. Although now they had more hostages.

The idiots kept sending in envoys. Jameson and crew kept capturing them and then tethering their ships in the *Moth's* wake. Why the convoy didn't leave she couldn't understand.

She'd made it clear after the consummation that she was no longer available. And once they made it to port and she could access an intergalactic bank, it would be official. She'd be out from under her father's thumb and an heiress to boot.

With a husband who couldn't stand to look at her until he was sunk to the hilt.

"Problems?" an accented voice asked.

Whirling from the observation window in the common recreation room, she noted the First Mate's wife. Michonne, a follower of the Dkar religion, had recently married someone outside her cast, just like Ghwenn. But at least Michonne's husband didn't scowl at his wife.

"What's it like having a husband who is agreeable?"

"You think Damon is agreeable?" Michonne snickered. "Maybe now he is, but not so long ago, he was the one being an ass about marriage."

"What changed?"

Michonne shrugged. "He finally figured out he was an idiot and came to his senses."

"I hear when your father took you captive Damon came to your rescue."

The other woman smiled. "He did."

"I don't know if Craig would." Given their new status, she'd stopped thinking of him by his last name and refused to use that horrible nickname. So she did something unexpected and used his actual given name. He hated it.

"Do you want him to save you?"

"He already did." Every day he didn't hand her over he rescued her. What she wanted was for her husband to stop pining over a dead woman and love the one right in front of him.

She must have been silent too long because Michonne nudged her.

"You just thought of something."

"Is it possible to love someone who hates you?"

"Crank doesn't hate you."

Perhaps not, but he hated the fact that Ghwenn made him forget. Why wouldn't he let Sky go? How could she remove his guilt once and for all?

What if... She had an idea. "I need to get off this ship."

"Are you going to make him think you've been kidnapped so he rescues you and declares his love? Because that was already done, and I'd rather not share that story." Michonne gave her a look.

"No, because, knowing Craig, he'd let me go and then be even more miserable convincing himself it was the right thing to do."

"Then what are you going to do?"

"Make him miss me." Show him what it was like without her.

Which could backfire, but at the same time, it was past time she stopped allowing herself to be used, and that included by her husband.

"What are you going to do?" Michonne asked. "Because that's a devious look in your eyes."

Which matched the devious plan in her heart.

And she hatched it the moment they hit the planet.

She kidnapped herself.

CHAPTER 17

"What do you mean she's gone?" Crank frowned at Zane. He'd sent the ensign to fetch Ghwenn from their room.

The ship had just docked, and the captain left to meet with their next client.

After much haggling, they'd just released the elves, with them promising to leave Ghwenn and the *Moth* alone. In return, the captain of the emerald ship parted with some of their precious maple syrup. An Earth commodity known as liquid gold. Bribery was alive and well in the galaxy.

But that didn't mean his pixie was safe.

"Sorry, Chief, er, sir, er..."

"Where the fuck is Ghwenn?" Crank barked. He tapped at his wrist, opening a communication channel. "Solanz, I need a location on my wife."

"Sorry, but her signal is not available at this time, Chief."

The words sent a cold spell through him. "Zane, where are the Driadalys ships?"

"They left, sir."

"When?" And when had Ghwenn last been seen?

No one could say for sure. The cameras last recorded her in his room. Sitting on the bed. Prim and perfectly attired. So unlike how she looked when in his arms with her lips passion swollen and her hair tousled.

There one moment, gone the next.

Impossible. Yet no matter how many times he re-ran the videos, the same thing appeared, which was to say nothing.

A sane man would have said good riddance. After all, he'd never wanted another wife. Never wanted to have the shell he'd built cracked. Never wanted to feel love again.

In the midst of pacing, he froze.

But the word still vibrated within.

Love.

Oh, fucking hell. I fell in love with her.

How had that happened? How could it happen?

Because...Ghwenn was amazing. Strong. Snooty. Vulnerable. Combative. Funny. Sexy.

And he'd been an asshole to her.

Because I love her. And it made him feel guilty. So he hurt her. Hurt the woman he loved, which was wrong.

Fuck. He was such a moron because it hit him then. Loving Ghwenn didn't mean he stopped loving Sky. He'd always love her. But the living couldn't be with the dead.

The realization shouldn't have been so shocking. But it was. Because Ghwenn was alive and gone and he needed her. Needed her back right now.

"Solanz, I need you to scan every single camera in that port. We have to find my wife." Who could be on an elf ship heading for home, and yet... This was just the kind of stunt he could see her pulling to force an epiphany.

Damn her. He'd shake her when he found her. Then kiss her. Then maybe shake her some more.

But how to find her?

There seemed to be no visual trail to follow. Not a hint.

He exited the ship and stood by the large bay doors as cargo was shuttled in for the wedding party. Big-ass fucking crates.

Had she hidden inside?

He pivoted to look, and yet something tugged him another way. Back toward the hangar. He passed by the ground crew busy schlepping around merchandise. He stalked through into the next warehouse. A quieter one, and yet this was where he needed to be. He could feel it.

He treaded lightly and found her. Sitting on a box. Legs tucked and hands clasped together.

"You ran away," he announced as he neared. Since the revelation of her lineage, she'd gone back to her natural colors. The dye in her hair was completely gone, the chopped ends curling a bit. The bright green strands framed her face as she tilted it.

Her green gaze met his. "I was giving you a choice."

"A choice to what?" he asked.

"Be with your ghost."

"A ghost doesn't keep my dick warm at night."

"There are appliances you can buy to rectify that."

"Don't need to buy shit. I've got a wife."

"That you never wanted."

"Maybe I changed my mind. Come home with me, pixie."

"I think I'm going to lose the contents of my stomach." The harshly spoken words emerged from behind him, and before Crank could whirl, they hit with force. *Don't move, machine man.*

His muscles froze.

"Father." Ghwenn's voice held aloof disdain. "What an unpleasant surprise. I thought you'd be planning your next wedding."

"Already in process."

"And yet you still found time to come after me?"

"It's not too late. Your trespasses will be forgiven if you return at once."

"Kind of you to offer, but unnecessary. I have a husband."

Crank's frozen mouth couldn't even form the words, *fucking right she does.* How emasculating.

"Husband?" There was clear sneering in the words. "Worse than a human, you chose a cyborg to sully your body."

"He's a good man."

"He's a biological host for a parasite. Hardly fit for a princess. Which is why I'll be doing you a favor when I kill him."

"No need. I'll come peacefully." She stood. "He doesn't want me."

Say what? Crank could only ogle as his pixie moved to leave with her father.

What was she thinking?

You'll soon be free, Craig.

But he didn't want to be free. He'd come to find her to explain that he loved her. But now this douche nozzle was getting in the way.

Taking away his wife.

The first time that happened, he was powerless to prevent it.

This time...he refused to allow it.

He twitched a finger. The compulsion hummed in him. *Don't move.*

Another muscle spasmed. A shudder went through his body. And he snapped.

Ghwenn had reached her father, a man with a triumphant sneer on his face.

"Don't you dare take my wife!" Crank roared and charged. Ended up going right through the hologram.

Staggering, he regained his balance and whirled to see Ghwenn smirking.

"He wasn't real," Crank stated.

She shook her head.

"This was all fake!" His voice rose.

She nodded.

"But the voice that froze me..." He'd been paralyzed.

"That was all you. Your bots that is. They helped."

His own nanotech betrayed him? "Why?" he growled.

"Because we were both tired of waiting for you to realize you loved me."

"Definitely don't like you after that stunt," he muttered, his brows drawn together in a frown.

"You were going to save me."

"Of course I was fucking was."

"Because..." she prodded.

"Because I fucking love your annoying little ass. Happy now? I tried to make sure you couldn't weasel your way in. Tried to stay in my deep wallow, but you just had to squirm your way in."

Her lips parted in a smile. "Was that so hard to admit?"

"Yes."

She approached him. "Poor cyborg."

"I can't believe my bots plotted against me."

"They tried to fix you, but in case you hadn't noticed, you're pretty stubborn."

"Just a tad."

"But so am I." She wrapped her arms around him. "It's why we make such a perfect pair."

"I ain't giving up my spot on the *Moth* just because you're a princess."

"I never asked you to. I am, however, renouncing my position as part of my father's court."

"You can quit?" he queried.

"Of a sort. I've taken steps to ensure my father will not bother us or your ship."

"You'd give up being a princess for me?" He couldn't stop his incredulity.

"Being a princess isn't as fun as it sounds."

"But what about your wealth?"

"For a man with the smarts of a machine, you're awfully dense at times. I'd give up anything for your love."

"But I thought elves didn't believe in it."

"I didn't until I became a certain cyborg's bride. I love you, Craig Abrams."

And for once he didn't have a grumpy retort. A hard cock, yes. A need for this woman, even more. He crushed her to him, his mouth seeking hers for a hot embrace. His hands tugged at her skirts, pulling them up that he might sink himself into her.

It didn't take him long to find his pleasure, and her right there with him, whispering, *Love you forever*.

Which, given their lifespan, could be a long time.

The ensign, however, that chose to interrupt them —"I found the chief and his wife."—would probably die.

Later.

He had some more apologizing to do first.

EPILOGUE

IT WAS ONLY when they were in their room a few hours later that her husband finally asked, "How does a princess resign? Isn't it like your birthright?"

"Royalty is decided by the purity of the bloodlines. And I am no longer pure."

"Because you're sleeping with a cyborg," he said with a sneer.

She rolled onto his chest and peered into his eyes wanting to see them when she said, "No, because I'm pregnant with one."

Good thing he was already lying down. His eyes rolled back in his head.

But he'd waken soon and then probably pass out when she mentioned it was twins.

She snuggled him. Her grumpy cyborg husband.

To her surprise, she heard his voice inside her head, *My pixie stowaway bride.* Together, forever.

THE ALLEY PROVED empty this time of night. Very little light shone, leaving it draped in shadows.

The stench of things rotting seeped from the very stone itself. The garbage collectors had obviously not been by in some days.

This most auspicious of locations was where the note indicated Kobrah Jameson should come.

A note written on scrap paper and one a sane man would have ignored. After all, he recognized the looping scrawl.

It was that familiarity that drew him from the safety of his ship, eschewing any guards as protection. Not even telling anyone but the *Moth* where he went.

A scuff had him whirling, facing the far end of the alley where the darkness hung deepest.

"Might as well come out. I know you're there."

He could feel it. An anticipation pulsing in his breast.

At first, he didn't even notice, so cleverly did the cloak conceal their presence. But as the person neared, he began to make out details. The tears in the fabric. The limp in the gait.

"Stop and show yourself." Because he had to be sure. His hand rested on the grip of his sidearm.

The figure halted. Lifted pale hands and pulled back a hood. Blonde hair pulled back taut. Bright blue eyes. Gaunt features with dark circles showing her fatigue.

She looked beaten. Tired. Yet she still drew him even after her betrayal.

"It's been awhile. Wife." He couldn't help that hard inflection, that reminder of what she'd done. She'd abandoned him. Without word. Without apology. Backstabbing him and the crew. Now, four EC years later, she thought she could just contact him out of the blue and...what? What did her note mean when she said, *Help us.*

Help who?

"Kobrah." She folded her hands over her stomach, keeping her gaze straight. "Thank you for coming."

"As if I wouldn't. I've been waiting for this moment." The gun left his holster and aimed at a spot between her eyes.

Going into the meeting he'd convinced himself he could do it. Kill the woman who'd betrayed him. Free himself to be with another.

Faced with her... She didn't plead for mercy. Didn't ask for forgiveness.

Someone else did. "Don't kill my mommy." A small figure darted from the shadows, wrapped herself around the woman's legs, and stared at him defiantly.

Bright blue eyes, light brown skin, and a mass of curls haloing her head.

A roaring white wave of shock hit Jameson as he gaped. He managed to stutter, "Who?"

Dara's chin angled higher. "Say hello to your daughter."

Stayed tuned for The Captain's Secret Daughter